CURSEBIRD ON A WIRE

The Alchemist's Agent: A Novella

E. M. BURNHAM

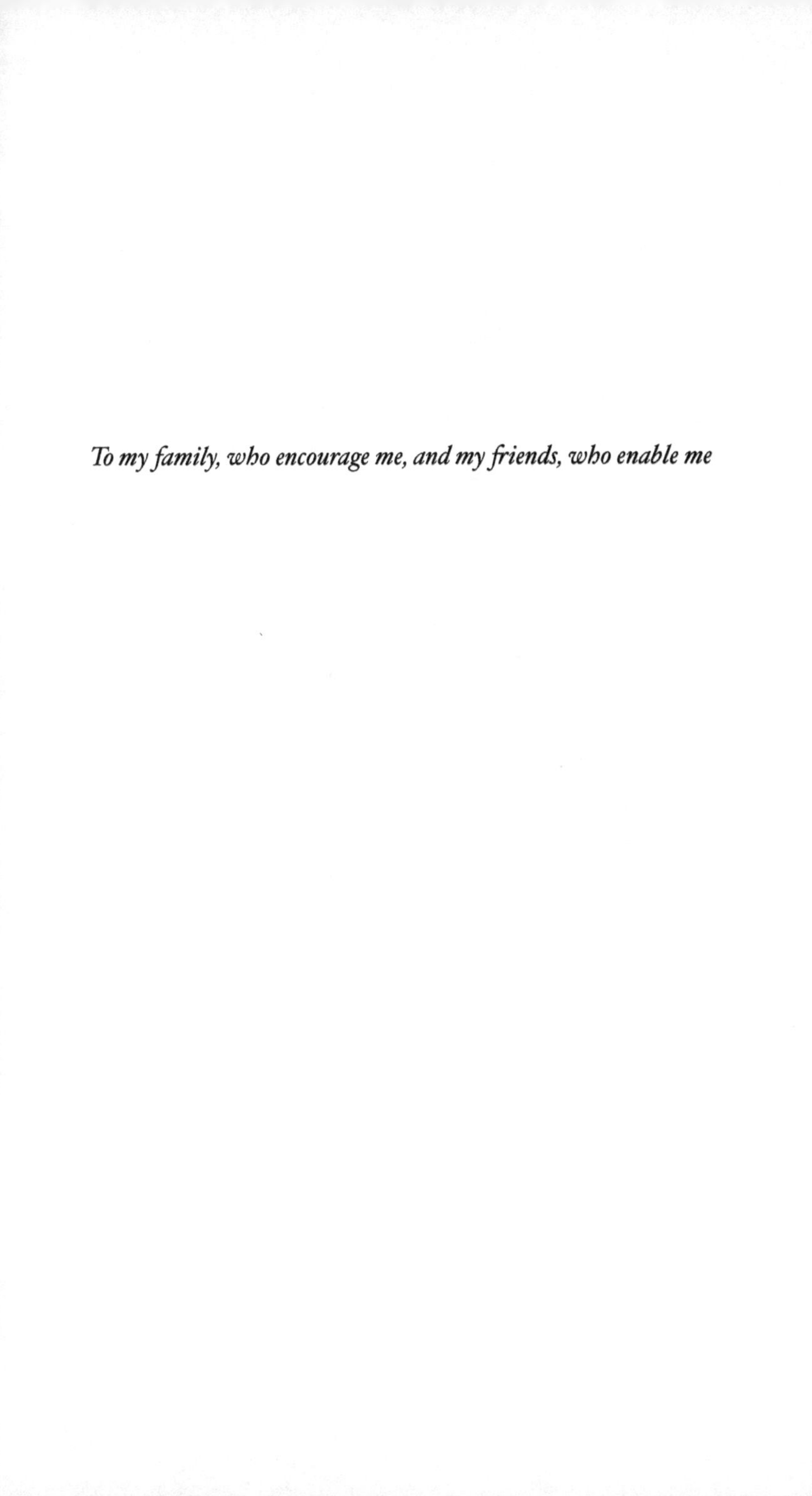

To my family, who encourage me, and my friends, who enable me

CONTENTS

CURSEBIRD ON A WIRE

Ibram rose early the morning of the party and shook out his clothes where he'd left them to air near the carved window screen that looked out onto the kitchen garden. The air smelled like warm bread and only faintly like the acrid stench of burnt sugar. It wasn't unpleasant, truth be told. He could just about hear the kitchen staff bustling down below. Most of Halfrey's male guards were still asleep, but when he glanced about, the beds of the night shift were empty.

He took a moment to stand there, in nothing but his underlinen and stockings, and breathe, even though his skin tingled in the cold. The silence felt deceptively peaceful. It almost seemed unreal, though he supposed after tonight he would know who to ask about that. Seven long months he'd spent keeping his head down and his mouth civil, working off the Halfreys' 'generosity' in allowing him out of their cells. He'd provided them with their pretense to approach Lady Azadiya and gain a foothold in Lityen. Cangsa, he'd even tried to catch the cursebird with the Halfrey's actual guardsmen when it had started battering itself to bits in the family courtyard.

He grinned down at his feet and wiggled his toes. The young Lord Halfrey had been driven mad by the cursebird and all its antics. Its malaise had spread itself thickly in three days. Small accidents at first, but every annoyance built over time. Clothes had been ruined, food burnt, and carefully packaged goods spoilt. Rot had consumed an entire root cellar since its appearance. Ibram had even taken a particularly long tumble down two flights of stairs—during a night patrol, but in full torchlight. Still, he didn't mind the bruises so much. Ama always said there was nothing like a bad fall to teach you how to land.

Ibram drew up his thick grey woolen breeches. Around him, the others began to stir. He threw on his cotton shirt and tucked it beneath his waistband.

"Still around, then?" his closest bunkmate Pall asked through a jaw-cracking yawn.

"My last day," Ibram said.

"You're the worst arm-for-hire I've ever met," Pall snorted. "You'd think a man as hungry for coin as you are might be able to recognize a windfall in your lap."

Laughter rippled out amongst the guards. Ibram shrugged. He could admit that soft work with a minor noble in a rich village was an attractive prospect no matter who you were, and even Ibram felt its pull. But folk who worked outside the imperial boundary set around alchemical sects never truly understood what living there meant for those inside it. He was only an arm-for-hire in the barest and most importantly legal sense of the term, after all. But Ibram kept his mouth shut. He'd spent the better part of their seven month journey not explaining the details of his erstwhile hiring; he wasn't going to come over all confessional now.

"I like to travel," he said, because he liked a good half-truth in place of a bald lie.

Pall sat up and stretched with a groan. Ibram walked to

the communal glass nailed to the wall. He brushed through his thick reddish-brown hair with both hands, curling the ends back behind his ears. He made a face and rubbed sleep out of the corners of his eyes and dragged his thumbs along his high cheekbones. He tilted his chin and scrubbed the back of his hand under his jaw. He never had much worry about a beard like Father, but he lived in hope. Twenty-three was as good an age to begin shaving as any.

Ibram returned to his cot. He picked up his heavy brown tunic, slashed with rust red at the shoulders and over the chest, and brushed the back down firmly with his hand. He'd been wearing it through the journey, but all it had needed last night was a good beating for dust and an airing. He shook it out before him and groaned; behind him, Pall laughed.

"Another unfortunate incident?" he called out in a fair imitation of Marshal Steward Pherick's choppy northern accent.

"I'm not upholding anyone's family honor in this."

Ibram held the tunic out before him and nodded. Pall laughed again. *His* clothing was perfectly fine, of course. Ibram took a closer look at his buttons. The knots that should have held his tunic closed on Ibram's right side hung loose on their threads. The night before they'd been as tight as the day he'd brought the garment home from the tailor's.

Ibram breathed out through his nose. He dropped the tunic onto his cot and then rubbed his thumbnail against his eyebrow. The damned Ruckus had done that, and on the *day* —Well, it couldn't be helped. A cursebird would have its way.

He frowned, standing still while all around him the Halfrey guards ran out the door to the sound of Cook's bell calling them to breakfast. The party was to begin late midday, and even if he wasn't of the household, he had to look better than a vagrant. Lady Azadiya would be attending, after all; he wanted to present a good impression to make up for his failure in the North.

He frowned. His belt wouldn't cover this, and he didn't have... He looked back towards his cot and the leather bag peeking out beneath it. He might have enough pins in his mending bag to hold the tunic together from the lining, but he could just imagine himself wincing every time he had to bow and a pin jabbed him for his trouble. He'd be bleeding out as soon as they opened the gates. Ibram sighed.

Five minutes later, with his old green and brown leather quilted gambeson in place and his broad leather belt wrapped around his stomach, he ran down the rickety wooden stairs where the guardsmen lived above the kitchens and across the servants' courtyard. Marshal Steward Pherick already had his little notebook in front of him and was scratching items off with the stick of red pigment he kept in a pouch.

He raised his eyebrows and ticked something off his list. "You're out of uniform, Ibram," he said curtly, and made an obvious survey of all the other guardsmen, resplendent as loafs of bread in a bakery.

Ibram bowed with his hands over his stomach. Marshal Steward Pherick was taller than him, which rankled, but many folk were. His slate grey hair hung in ragged layers over his narrow head and dangled past his shoulders. He, at least, had managed to put on his feast day best clothes, a long rust-color tunic and brown breeches edged in complicated golden thread. The marshal steward huffed and waved him up. Ibram placed a hand on his sica to stop it swinging against his leg.

"Yes, Marshal Steward," Ibram said. He tugged on his woolen sleeves. "I had...a bit of an accident."

He whistled a short birdcall, and Marshal Steward Pherick winced. Everyone had been made uneasy when the Ruckus had screamed about the manor, a small red bird made of bleeding bell petals and rusty iron splinters with eyes that dripped ink. It had beat its wings against the walls and its head into the doors until it collapsed in a sulfurous stink and disintegrated. The general consensus was that the cursebird had been sent by a competitor, but the small noble houses in Lityen were more cautious than in other parts of the province. They lived in the shadow of an alchemist sect, after all, and had learned to measure success in different ways. Yet small accidents had begun to pile up almost immediately and guard duties had been doubled. Lord Sans had decreed his exhibition would continue regardless.

Marshal Pherick sighed heavily and tapped his pigment stick. "And this was unrepairable?" he asked.

Ibram nodded. "It was fine in the night and ruined by morning," he said.

Lally, one of the lowlanders they'd picked up on the way down from Halfrilat, noticed him. She grinned widely, showing off her gold tooth. She slapped the shoulder of the guard next to her and gestured in Ibram's direction. Ibram pretended not to notice.

"He won't like it," Marshal Pherick said.

"I'll dip in the back, sir," Ibram said. "It won't matter once the guests arrive."

"You know perfectly well you're placed in the reception hall," the Marshal said, in as close to a peevish tone as Ibram had ever heard from him. They were only a small grouping, barely forty in all, and even with all the recent hires, it was the barest respectable minimum. A party like this meant all hands to the pump, including Ibram. Well, no one had asked him, to be sure, but it had been heavily implied. Everything had to be just so for Lord San's introduction to Lityen society.

Ibram spread his hands. "I've got a bit of brown on me, though, haven't I? And I'm only employed for today. Stick me behind a stack of presents and no one will notice the difference."

Marshal Pherick pinched the bridge of his nose and then waved Ibram off. "Go and eat your breakfast," he muttered. There were red fingerprints to either side of his nose, but Ibram kept it to himself.

He sat down to eat his bowl of brown butter quash and his cup of unsweetened, unstrained black shay while Marshal Steward Pherick stood at the head of the long trestle table and ran through their security duties again. Lord Sans was nervous about everything from the food to the crockery to the new servants to the possibility of anonymous rogue competitors sabotaging his delicacies, especially the ice wine and the alchemy which protected it. The Ruckus hadn't helped his paranoia. The young lord had lost half his wardrobe and a full third of the household goods his father had put in his pack train. Ibram chewed and swallowed his mush carefully and kept his eyes down. Repairing the damage would take a chunk out of the common budget.

There was grumbling from the others when Marshal Steward Pherick loudly reminded them that Ibram was to guard the lordship's presentation table during the entry processional. It was an honor usually reserved for household guards, and Ibram was merely an arm-for-hire. Lally thumped him for it, presumably out of Northern solidarity, since she was to be at the table alongside him. Ibram merely elbowed her back, and ate his breakfast while Marshal Steward Pherick continued. As the morning led on, they assembled for what Pherick called his "fools' trials" with all the servants who were going to be serving in the public courtyard and those ferrying food and drink from the kitchens. They each lined up to practice for the party, carrying trays and offering the guards chosen to play guests fake cups of wine. The new servants were mostly locals, though none that Ibram recognized, and hastily employed for the business. It took a lot to get a proper merchant's showing up and running, and they'd lost a great deal of time.

The practice was lively, and smooth walking for the first thirty minutes. Then two full trays of wooden bowls fell to the ground as if the servants carrying them were pushed, and no one would own up to it. The guards grew watchful even as they tripped on the increasingly churned up ground, and a washerwoman lost an entire tray of melon spoons to the mud underneath the walking platform that lined the courtyard; no one was small enough to get them out. Ibram accepted an empty cup from a sweating waiter, and smiled encouragingly. Behind him, something rather large crashed to the ground.

"It's fine!" Lally yelled in her thick Northern croak. "It's just the linens!"

The servant turned pale and rushed past Ibram, who turned at the waist to watch them all scurry. He saw half of the cloth meant for the dainty mouths of Halfrey's guests crumpled on the grass before the entire table was overtaken by a swirling mass of brown robed servants. He chuckled into the back of his hand and then shrugged when some of the other guards glared.

He turned back around in time to see Marshal Steward Pherick sigh heavily and look over his notebook.

"Again!" he called out, and guards and servants—those not running for the laundry—took up position.

❦

The guards were soon released for morning patrols, so Ibram spent some time in relative quiet, patrolling the outside of the manor and making sure no stall seller attempted to set up shop again. At near midday, he sat along the high second walkway with the other guards. Staring down into the six-sided courtyard was like peering down into the beehive it was named for; servants dispatched huge platters of milk bun puddings and bowls of honey out the doors, and collected tray upon tray of all the fruit that could be taken from the market: star-shaped syah berries, bowls of cubed melon in syrup, and glass apples piled up in great glimmering pyramids. A gigantic basket of rolls made Ibram's stomach grumble in yearning. There were yellow grain salads studded with nuts, platters of clarifying bowls of broth, and even six entire wheels of cheese that had been cut into scenes of Northern life.

Lally nudged his shoulder. "Let me see your sica," she said.

"I'm not that kind of boy, young mistress," Ibram said.

Lally groaned and held out her calloused hand. "Disgusting," she said.

Ibram drew his sica, and handed it over hilt-first. "Careful," he said. "That was a gift."

Lally held the inwardly curved dagger so that the blade caught the light. She whistled. "It's a wicked thing," she said, and tossed it in her hand.

"Westerners are all wicked," Ibram said. "The only difference between us and Easterners is direction."

Lally snorted, and pointed with the blade down below. "I think that one looks like the compound at Halfrilat," she said.

"You've never seen that," Ibram muttered.

She handed him back his sica. "Well, am I right?"

Ibram sheathed it. He squinted at the serving platters. "It looks like a mound of shredded cheese next to a pile of little toasts."

Lally sighed extravagantly. "You have the imagination of a tarmap."

"Fine enough." Ibram rolled his eyes. Northern manors were built like rounded hills attached by tunnels to keep in the heat. "It looks like a haystack which might—somehow—remind me of Lord Sans' ancestral home. It's not as tall, though, and I don't think I'd enjoy sleeping in it."

"I take it back," Lally said. "A tarmap would make a better storyteller."

"They make better eating, too," Ibram said.

Cook rang the bell twice, and they rolled to their feet along with the other guards to head down the stairs. Staff lined up around the trestle tables for dinner, sour buns filled with dripping and mushrooms and a mug of small beer. There was no room around them to sit this time, with almost the entire household prepping for the night's festivity.

Ibram wandered off to sit on the wooden platform for a bit of elbow room and some air. His stomach fluttered, but the beer tasted all right, and the roll was soft. He chewed and swallowed with his eyes on the eaves of the wooden portion of the roof. Here in the servants' section, there was no protective glass ceiling, and the main grounds were exposed to the open air. The wind felt good on his face when he tilted it upwards.

He blinked at the grey sky. It might be the Ruckus made it rain, next, or cracked the ceiling so all the wine decanted for the party spoiled with drips. He licked his lips and took another bite. Probably not—well, possibly yes—but the Ruckus was more annoying than anything, nothing but an irritant, really. He'd had non-alchemical bad luck that was worse. It was the party that had everyone on edge. Lord Sans had been ordered by his father to encourage trade, after all, and he couldn't become the toast of Lityen society without a party.

Gravy seeped onto Ibram's hands. He licked them clean and then bent down to dry them on the grass. Around him, the whole house was bustling into party order, servants gathering up the rented serviceware and last trays of food and guards finding their patrolling partners. A stray knee knocked into him from behind and he tumbled down off the platform.

Ibram tucked his head and rolled into a clear patch with a groan as his boots thudded into the dirt. He pushed himself to his feet. "Kivan the Red take you!"

Lally cackled as she ran by, closing her thin blonde braid into a bun with those jeweled clasps the Northerners favored as she disappeared into the family courtyard. Ibram straightened his clothes as he brushed himself off, and then bent down to pick up his plate and cup. He knocked dirt off his low-heeled boots against the walkway and walked over to drop his dishes into the communal tub at the end of the trestle table. Ibram rolled his neck along his shoulders and then gripped his shoulder where his half-cloak connected to his gambeson. He stopped and stared back up to the male guards' room. He'd *forgotten* his half-cloak.

A servant stood up, hefting a massive tray full of delicately stacked glass bowls for the fruit wines, and wavered on the steps up from the huge wash basins set out on the kitchen garden. She tottered sideways, glass tinkling alarmingly, and then right as the glittering tower leaned heavily left. Ibram lunged forward with both hands raised and caught the stack. They both froze, wide eyes staring at each other over the dessert dishes. The laughing servants around them stilled.

"Slowly," the servant mouthed, and Ibram nodded.

He braced the bowls as she took a step forward and then another careful step until the tray and glass dishes were again in full balance. At her nod, Ibram let his hands drop. He breathed a sigh of relief.

The tray wavered, the servant shrieked, and Ibram snatched a tumbling bowl out of mid-air. The other top three shattered with an alarmingly musical tonality.

He held the survivor up by the rim. "Does it need to be washed again?"

"Olla!" yelled Cook. Her broad florid face was turning a worrying shade of maroon. "Get over there and help your sister! I swear, I'm carving every plate you break out of your bones!"

Another servant girl ran up from the wash tub and grabbed the end of her sister's tray. Ibram stretched himself upwards and replaced his captured bowl on top of the stack; he stood to one side as the servants carefully made their way up the steps to the right-hand side of the wooden platform. A cough burst out to his left; he turned and there stood Marshal Steward Pherick. Immediately, Ibram's back went stiff.

He bowed with his hands on his stomach. "Apologies, sir," he said.

Marshal Steward Pherick sighed as Ibram straightened. "No need," he said. "If that's the worst of what we get during this event, I'll take it and be glad."

Ibram nodded dutifully.

He stood back and tucked his left hand around the hilt of his dagger where it was strapped to his waist. Marshal Steward Pherick sighed again; he was a man for long faces and schedules. He ticked off another mark on his list, and the pigment snapped in half. Ibram bit both lips together and swallowed back his laughter while Pherick grumbled and held both arms out, pad in one hand and crumbling pigment in the other.

"Oh, hang...here, take this," Marshal Steward Pherick said, and thrust the paper into Ibram's chest. Ibram fumbled the pad, caught it, and held his arms out stiffly so that no crumb of pigment smeared his gambeson. Marshal Pherick carefully poured his broken stick into his pouch and clapped his hands over the railing; red crumbs flew into the air. He jerked his head towards the servants' door and walked off. Ibram followed.

He handed the marshal back his property as they stepped

from the rough planks to the painted wood of the family courtyard. Ibram winced a little to look at it; the servants hadn't been able to clean the place after all. The garden in the center of the courtyard here was for pleasure (and medicine, as he recalled it; the Lady Vo Messyn had been a well-respected doctor), but he doubted Lord Sans had much use for it. He was a small man in every sense of the word except height, with shining blond hair and wide-set eyes. He'd spent the first day of their occupation decapitating honey-lamps until the whole border was raw stems. Now, he paced up and down the stone path, throwing bits of bread into the drained fountain splashed with red dye (and still vaguely smoking for some reason) while a servant followed behind with a tray. At least all the young lord's buttons looked done up.

Marshal Pherick and Ibram stepped down the little stone staircase and bowed before Lord Sans, who tossed the remains of his meal back onto his servant's tray and held both arms and palms out at his waist perfunctorily. He curled his hands closed, and they unbent.

"Is everything prepared?" Lord Sans demanded. He frowned. "Marshal Pherick, you've got..." he trailed away and gestured vaguely at his face. "Is it paint? Are you ill? Clean your nose, man, we're trying to make a good impression!"

The Marshal Steward's face went slack, and his hand jerked up to his face. He glanced at his fingertips and then narrowed his eyes at them. Carefully, he withdrew a handkerchief and cleaned his face and hands again.

Lord Sans waved away the servant at his shoulder and rocked back and forth on his heels. He pulled down his gambeson and brushed down the front. "Trida tells me we lost the use of the linen. What are my guests to use instead? The table sheets? The—what are *you* wearing?"

Ibram tucked his arms behind his back. To be fair, he thought his green and brown made a prettier sight with his grey breeches than Lord Sans' house coloring. Rust and brown wasn't the ugliest combination Ibram had ever seen, but it was high in the lists, even with a fancy example in front of him. That high up in the mountains, you'd think they'd want a little more color in their lives.

"There was a small problem with the laundry, lordship," Marshal Pherick answered for him. "But nothing to disturb the course of the festivities."

Lord Sans groaned and shook his open palms to the sky. "What did I do to deserve this?" he muttered.

He twisted on his heels and began walking. Ibram looked to the Marshal Steward.

"Yes, my lord," Marshal Steward Pherick said as he gestured to Ibram to come along. He glanced down at his pad. "I've been through the lists with the cooks as well as the guards. Even the recent hires have practiced their roles."

"And the food looks well?" Lord Sans asked. He turned the corner near the walking platform and began to pace on the graveled walkway. "The wine has been decanted? The ale?"

"I oversaw their placement myself, my lord," Marshal Steward Pherick said. "Everything is in order."

"And the centerpieces? What about the ice wine?"

"What with all the disturbances, I thought it best to give it its own guard, my lord. It's still within the casks, but they've been placed nearest to your doorway so that the guests may anticipate their taste."

"And if they don't?" Lord Sans sighed with his entire body and looked up towards the glass roof that covered the court-yard. The young lord was nineteen if he was a day, the bird-like third son in a family of ten, each one of whom more closely resembled a rachtbear than the last. Ibram felt a little sympathy for him, if only just. It was tough work to make your fortune so far from home, but the lordship's hard landing if he failed—if that were possible—was still a feather bed. Ibram looked around at the thick splashes of red ink that stained the family courtyard and wrinkled his nose at the spreading patches of orange grass near the walkway. The Vo Messyns' land marshal was not going to be pleased when the family retook the manor.

"Lityen loves a party, lordship," Ibram said. "Even more than the river folk. And no one's been able to bring ice wine down this far yet. You'll get a good payday out of this, mark me."

Wines from the North were always bound to cause a bit of a stir; they were difficult to transport without spoiling. The grapes were started in underground springs with sun charms, then frozen when they were ripe. The stuff was too rich and sweet for Ibram's taste, if he was being honest. Give him a good glass of apple cider or his ama's homebrewed tolnic any day. Northern wines were difficult to acquire, though, which was like waving gold in an evening courtyard for nobility if Ibram was any judge. The Halfreys were the first family to try to make a go of the difficult journey in three generations. The ice wine alone would have brought guests to the party, given the rumors around what just one dram did for the constitution.

"It's not just about the money," Lord Sans insisted. "Not *everything* is about gold and silver, you know."

That was true enough, Ibram supposed. Some things could be about copper, after all. He bowed because he couldn't think of anything to say without laughing. He heard the clink of trays and glasses as the servants began walking along the upper walkways that led to the two doors into the public courtyard. As he straightened, he watched Marshal Steward Pherick make the conscious decision not to tell his now slowly simmering lordship about the little bumps in the road during practice.

He touched the little leather wallet attached to his belt where he kept his bells and dice to call upon Yilka the Green. There was no need to seek her aid, of course, but he'd fallen into the habit when the Halfrilat guards had stripped him down. They'd been returned with courtesy when Lord Halfrey had cleared the air between him and Ibram, but it had still been jarring.

"Then they all know what to do in case anything goes astray?" Lord Sans asked. He twisted the fingers of his right hand.

Ibram snorted and quickly turned it into a cough, covering his lower face with his elbow. Lord Sans looked back over his shoulder with a frown on his narrow mouth. Ibram tucked his arms behind his back and stood quietly. His toes began to tap in his boots, but he brought them under control.

"And you, Uncleton," Lord Sans said. His pale green eyes narrowed. "You brought—you're certain your...friend will be here? The Lady Hobon?"

Ibram didn't roll his eyes, but it was very near thing. "Ucalegon, Lordship," he said. "I gave her acceptance to Marshal Steward Pherick myself."

Lord Sans scratched his carefully trimmed blond beard. The Halfreys had been very surprised a lowly arm for hire was in contact with an alchemist, much less a titled one. The discovery had sent him straight to the dungeon while they decided if he were a spy or not, but it had to be admitted that her employment had kept him from actually being convicted. Laumye the Blue turned all tides eventually, Ibram reminded himself.

The most gracious Northern lord, Lord Halfrey himself, had decreed that Ibram could keep all the money in his pockets and his very own wrists out of shackles for the price of a little humiliation and one noble invitation. Thus he could be considered paid for his 'inconveniencing' in Halfrilat, and as far as Lord Halfrey and his son were concerned, that was an end to hard feelings. Who was Ibram to say he knew better than they?

"And which preceptory is she from?" he asked.

Ibram grit his teeth to hold back a very loud sigh; they'd been through this so many times. "She is of the Preceptory of Yseult, Lordship. Their discipline covers the physical body."

Lord Sans began to grin slyly, and Ibram fixed his eyes on the far wall of the courtyard behind him. What a lovely mural of...some kind of farming procedure. "There are seven such preceptories within the sect," he attempted to explain yet again. "Mariae, where sits the Lord Preceptor. Afsoun, who seek to understand the transmutation of objects. Bedris—"

"Perhaps I should have sent my own message," Lord Sans muttered. "A written invitation from someone far closer in status..."

"She wouldn't have accepted," Ibram interrupted right back, but softened his tone. No need to remind anyone that any Lady Hobon was so far above a young lord birthed in a snowdrift that she'd have to squint to see him. "She's a Merrilian."

Well, he could hint.

Lord Sans squinted at him; he still didn't recognize the province, even though Marshal Steward Pherick had spent half their journey from the Bright Broken Peaks down to the garden provinces grilling Ibram on the main houses and persons of note in Lityen for Lord Sans' edification. With a blank face, Marshal Steward Pherick began to climb Mount Ignorance again. "She's of the West, my lord. Introductions to strangers are complicated."

Lords Sans nodded. Ibram glanced at the Marshal Steward, who inclined his head in slight approval. It was important for the young lord to know these things, even if he seemed incapable of remembering it most days. To be...fair,

Ibram supposed the confusion wasn't totally Lord Sans' fault. Lityen, for all its imperially restricted size, was a fairly traditional alchemists' domain, and thus a bit of an oddity compared to the rest of the Vissilian Empire. The high and the low mixed together, the shops and stalls crowded with petitioners, and all brought within touching distance because of the alchemists atop the living mountain.

"The West," Lord Sans scoffed. "Such..." He puckered his lips and eyed the trail of servants as they scurried by. Young Olla tripped again, but recovered, and he winced. "She won't eat with her fingers, will she?"

Ibram clenched his jaw and forced himself to relax again. In only a few small hours, he would be free of this petty noble and his family's machinations. He just had to keep himself calm in the meantime. The West had been the last of the conquered lands before the Grassland Expansion, and its customs remained a bit farther from the Imperial Vissilian norm than many found strictly comfortable. The North had been among the first, and the great houses had done enough intermarrying that you could throw a pebble and strike some castoff Imperial cousin lurking in the family bloodline.

Marshal Steward Pherick coughed. "The Western practice is family-oriented, my lord," he said. "Amongst strangers they use cutlery."

"I doubt Lady Azadiya will forget whose party she's at, Lordship," Ibram said.

Lord Sans frowned.

"My Lord," Marshal Steward Pherick said, smoothing his hand down his velvet robe. "Perhaps we should move into the receiving room?"

Lord Sans looked startled, which wasn't very new, but eager, which was a rather recent development. Ibram had spent hours riding alongside his carriage, carefully naming all the great houses in Lityen so that Marshal Steward Pherick could make note of their importance. Lord Sans had spent that time asking about the evening courtyards in the village, and naming various 'facts' about barbarians he'd learned from traveling shows. If he was successful, Ibram figured the young lord was counting on becoming an upstanding light of Lityen's social life as its shining Wit.

"Yes, yes, they'll be arriving soon, won't they?" Lord Sans tucked his long blond hair behind both ears and straightened his satin tunic. His flat cheekbones were flushed, but the rest of his face was pale. He flapped his right hand irritably and walked off.

They followed Lord Sans, and the servants tucked themselves against the walls to avoid obstructing the lord's path. Each courtyard was connected by four doors, two at the ground level and two on the upper level. The Vo Messyn manor was of recent construction, not built for defense; instead of enclosed towers for archers, the upper level was bracketed by open-air staircases and delicate balconies. The terraces that led further into the apartments and sitting rooms were equally dainty. As they walked past, Lally detached from her station on the wall and fell in at their rear.

It was a bit like being surrounded by sunflowers. Lord Sans and Marshal Steward Pherick wore their hair long and loose to their shoulders, held back at the ears with bejeweled iron clasps. Lally's more practical braid was tucked into a bun. Ibram had never adopted the fashion. He was smaller than all three and wore his dark hair short, as a Southerner might, but not shorn so close, a compromise between his Western mother and Vissilian father. They passed through the elaborate double doors that separated the family's apartments from the public courtyard, and Lord Sans sighed.

"At least it didn't attack here," he said. "I think Father would have damned me to oblivion if the entire manor was a loss."

"Yes, my lord," Marshal Steward Pherick replied.

Lally fell back to Ibram's side and raised her eyebrows at him. Ibram shrugged. He and the others had run from the family courtyard to the kitchen area and back again trying to catch the damnable little bird before it had exploded. The doors to the public courtyard, however, had been firmly shut, and the Ruckus had run out of steam before it could get through.

Ibram took careful stock of his surroundings as they walked. The public courtyard—far more elaborate and stately, with a cascading interior garden whose blooms hadn't faced execution—did look untouched. Each little open-air octagonal pavilion was arrayed in a different selection of Halfrey wares, complete with food and enough spare serviceware to cover any mishaps. As they passed, a servant was restacking a pyramid of buns while another rubbed dirt off one with a clean rag. They bowed as they passed and the girl lost both rag and bread to a stray elbow. Ibram bit his lip as they walked on.

"Are we certain the gift is suitable?" Lord Sans asked as they reached the reception hall.

"It will soon be the Festival of the Founder," Marshal Steward Pherick replied. "Considering that this is your lordship's introduction to Lityen, your entire party may be considered a part of the gift. A certain simplicity in the final offering is required."

Ibram stayed quiet even though that was absolutely untrue. The Festival of the Founder was the lessening of austerity following the Feast of the Sundered Legion; it signaled excess and dancing, and gifts without number. In the North, house gifts were typically food. The central provinces were usually more craft-based. In Lityen, house gifts were woodcraft, denoting the rich forests that crowded their half of the province. As an example of hopeful compromise, they'd decided on boiled wine sweets in small carved boxes. The trestle tables pushed to one side contained swirling pyramids of the things, more than enough for the expected throng, which was good since the first three batches of the candies had met fiery ends out the back of the servants' courtyard.

They walked through the great double doors that guarded the one entrance to the public courtyard and into the empty reception hall, warmed through with candles on every available sconce and a few sailing lights that had drifted in from the public courtyard. Lord Sans arranged himself at the head of the nearest table on the small wooden dais with Marshal Steward Pherick on his right and Lally and Ibram behind the gifts, more for show than any real security. The gifts would be formally presented to the guests as they left. To either side of the elaborately carved entrance gate stood two other members of the guard and beyond that a platoon of servants.

"Where's your half-cloak?" Lally whispered.

"Oh *hang*—" Ibram snapped his mouth closed as the filigree inner gate rose and the procession of guests began. He put his hands behind his back and stood straight.

As the reception line began, the hall grew hot. The early crowd was a bit larger than expected and hummed in anticipation. Several sly eyes glanced around to the rafters and the floor, and Ibram exchanged a quick look with Lally. Someone had absolutely spilled the water when the servants had been let out to gather food for the party. Ibram wondered who it was. He, of course, had been strictly discreet when running about his old haunts on his errands for the Marshal Steward. Lityen was a practical sort of place, and took curses seriously. After all, they made for excellent gossip.

Ibram saw several young lords and ladies from the more important families wander in with their assorted maids. He could see folk representing the Polis, the Tyal, the Vo Char and the Vo Wolly. The Vo Wolly were represented in force tonight; they had sent at least three of their largest boys. In turn, they were trailed by maids who all already seemed to be walking with sore feet and uncertain tempers. But then, the younger Vo Wolly set were like that. Ibram wondered how long it would take one of them to get lost in a hedge maze or upend a table.

He shifted on his own feet. Not everyone had followed the fashion of a short half-cloak on the right shoulder, but it was a close thing. He kept his face still and his eyes watchful. He didn't recognize most of them—some he remembered as his own family's customers—but from the satins and silks and snowy linen, he was certain their lines of Imperial credit ensured they kept a good cellar. The Festival of the Founder demanded it. Ibram smirked. It was practically a law to get drunk and toast to the old man's ascendancy into...well, history, at least. Ibram didn't quite see how inventing the imperial drainage system could propel an alchemist into the heavens, but he wasn't in charge.

There wasn't much to do but stand by the house gifts and look solemn. Guests walked past in a long train. It looked like the novelty of northern wine had drawn in a good crowd after all. The noise became louder in the antechamber as more guests began to arrive and their servants scuttled around to divest them of their coats and cloaks. Spring held full sway in Lityen, which meant rain and winds still edged with cold. Beside him, he felt Lally lean in more closely.

"Are we going to see your family here, young lord?" she whispered.

"I'm just an arm-for-hire," Ibram whispered back as he kept an eye on Marshal Steward Pherick. "All I did—"

Marshal Steward Pherick cleared his throat and they shut up. Lally stepped back into her place further down the table as the contract men began to file into the room, following whatever house they served and ready to jot down their young lords and ladies' preferences for consultation later.

Lords Sans nodded his head or bowed as the guests' servants introduced their employers, while Marshal Steward Pherick made note of their names in his gilded ledger. Ibram twitched his nose at the sharp sugary odor of the wine sweets in their boxes in front of him. He idly listened to the snippets of conversation, guests remarking on the amount of presents and what they hoped the Halfreys had sent for trade. Some even openly speculated on what stabilizing charms they'd used to get the stuff as far as Lityen at all. As the noise in the antechamber decreased, the sounds of the party in swing began to grow louder. Lord Sans began to look irritable, and his bows grew more perfunctory as time stretched. Ibram watched the young lord turn and say something sharply to Marshal Steward Pherick that made the man's entire face twitch.

"You get paid even if your lady doesn't show her face, right?" Lally whispered.

"She's an alchemist, not a puppy," Ibram said and ducked his face in her direction. "I can't just dangle a ribbon in front of her and get her to jump!"

"Don't alchemists down South like to take a personal interest in the world?" she asked.

He watched the line of party guests weave out into the antechamber. It was already long enough that his feet ached in anticipation. The back of his head prickled; his toes began to tap in their boots. Lord Halfrey had practically slavered at the chance for an introduction to a 'southern alchemist.' In the North, they were ascetics, mostly concerned with the nature of alchemy and content to rest on their one achievement: cantrips of ice. It took a chisel to get them out of their preceptories. The further down a body traveled, though, the more involved in daily life an alchemical sect became. Lityen, the last true settlement before the Imperial road west, followed the alchemical calendar more closely than any directive from the Empire. Festivals took up most of the year, promising hefty trade for anyone willing to live there with the close eye the Empress, Gracious and Divine, kept on her most...ebullient subjects.

"We're not in the South," Ibram said.

"Close enough!" Lally said with a grin. "Don't they drink? Even ours like a good ale now and again, and with all your talk, I thought it would be like watching two age-old friends running into each other's arms in a tearful reunion or something."

Heat crept up the back of Ibram's neck. "I never said anything like that!"

"Well, don't tell the Marshal Steward, he's a romantic."

Marshal Steward Pherick cleared his throat. They returned to their posts. Lally's grin was entirely unprofessional, and Ibram resented it.

Partway through the reception hour, Lady Sebbina, the Imperial commissioner, made her appearance. It was almost as important for her to be seen at the party as it was for Lady Azadiya in Lord Sans' estimation. No trade could be accomplished unless the Bureau of Commerce provided the appropriate seals and allowances, nor could Lord Sans stay in Lityen without the proper documents. He was lucky to be so far down in the line of succession back home, really. A minor noble house always had better luck in establishing themselves near alchemists.

Ibram supposed that, since she had accepted the invitation, the Halfreys' application was soon to be authorized. Her presence certainly interested the other guests immensely. She was just as Ibram remembered her, if a little more bent with age. Her light brown skin was lined with wrinkles at the eyes and mouth. Her white hair was twisted up underneath her pink cap, which was embroidered with white and blue flowers with mirrors in their centers. Her dress, also a deep pink, was long enough to hide her boots and her silk over-gown was thick with embroidered green vines. The heavy thunk of her engraved walking cane instinctively made him stand taller, as if she were about to yell at him to stop playing in the road and let her carriage through. The empty spot on his right shoulder where his half-cloak should have hung tingled.

Her sharp dark eyes passed over the table, Lally, and then himself without pausing. Her lips pursed as she walked by, her two servants sweeping past in her wake, and Ibram took a slow deep breath in and then held it. Oh, if the Ruckus struck Lady Sebbina they were all going to be in a great deal of trouble. He rubbed sweat from his palms off on his thighs. Was it a good thing or a bad thing to be back, after all?

Marshal Steward Pherick made the introductions as the two nobles bowed to each other. Lord Sans' hands were placed on his stomach, of course, while Lady Sebbina reached out with her arms. He turned his head at a sudden outburst of commotion from the antechamber, but nothing came of it except for a new influx of guests. Most of them were from the village, but Ibram saw a number of river and farm folk in their best lace and sturdy headdresses. Some of the guests were from the Western trading families down from Emerald Mountains, draped in clan beads and embroidered satins. A few older tradesfolk acknowledged Ibram with a short nod or by tapping a particular jewelry piece made by his family as they passed. He heard Lally snort once or twice, but Ibram didn't let himself do more than stand and guard. Being too familiar wasn't professional, after all.

The lights in the reception hall began to turn orange, signaling the approaching end of the hour. Ibram's breath stalled briefly in his throat, and he coughed to clear it. He looked carefully out of the corner of his eye at the Marshal

Steward and Lord Sans. The young lord's face was beginning to flush unfavorably in the warming light. Ibram shifted his gaze back to the dwindling trickle of guests in front of him.

Well. If she didn't come, it wasn't like he hadn't fulfilled his end of their coercive bargain. Lord Sans and his wares were out of the North safely with plenty of prospective customers amongst the guests tonight—Lady Sebbina herself liked a good cup at dinner! A tacit understanding was no kind of contract, and he hadn't even bled on anything, so it wasn't as if the Halfreys could claim he left a promise uncompleted. He rested his hand on his dagger as a pair of maids swept past behind Master and Mistress Tarsis.

He blinked. The Tarsises? He swallowed a laugh. They had actually come! He turned his head to watch them approach Lord Sans, who now resembled a piebald peach. Ibram elbowed Lally.

"Can you believe this?" he whispered.

"What?" she asked.

"They're *competitors*," he hissed in delight.

Her elbow knocked into his own ribs. "Why did they get an invitation, then?"

Ibram shrugged. "I couldn't say. Must have been in that last batch they sent me out with. Do you think lordship's face is going to be permanently that color?"

"Shh!" Lally said. The noise level hadn't gone down far enough that they could hear the main dais without straining.

"Master and Mistress Tarsis, welcome," Lord Sans said. They both bowed stiffly, though the Tarsises straightened only after Lord Sans. Mistress Tarsis' red hair trailed over her shoulders in ringlets, held back with a gauze scarf tied at the nape of her neck. Her husband's gold-embroidered skull cap twinkled in the light. They both wore blue sleeveless kaftans held closed by wide embroidered purple belts, following the Imperial fashion for married persons to complement each other's clothes. Lord Sans' brown and rust made him look like a cave sparrow next to them.

Master Tarsis touched his fingers to his lips and then turned his open palm out. With both hands, he signed to Mistress Tarsis and then nodded to Lord Sans. His wife—who was a lowland Northern transplant herself, now that Ibram thought about it—stepped forward.

"My husband hears, but cannot speak. We believe you do not sign, lordship," she said, rather than asked, loudly enough that Ibram didn't need to strain to hear her. Several other guests still to be greeted looked bemused.

Lord Sans cleared his throat. "I do not, Mistress," he replied. Mistress Tarsis nodded, and Lord Sans shifted his weight from one foot to the other. "I regret I must rely on your help."

"Not at all," she said. "Your surprising but gracious invitation gives my husband and myself a wealth of joy, lordship. We're always eager to sample the simple joys of my childhood home."

This introduction to local society was going brilliantly. A minor Polis hid her mouth behind her hand and ducked her head. Lally elbowed Ibram, and he elbowed her right back without turning around.

Lord Sans grunted. "As I hope to acquire some of your famous Southern vinegar."

Marshal Steward Pherick's face froze into blankness. Ibram kept himself from wincing, but only just. The South was famous for its red vinegar as it was for the thick heady wines that sprung from the same grapes, but there was no way anyone in the room thought the young lord wanted a sample of either. It was a bit of foolishness. Master Tarsis was from Vissilia itself, broad-bodied and dark-skinned, successful even without a house of any great note. Slowly, Pherick made an obvious note in his ledger, and then returned to staring out towards the entrance from over Lord Sans' shoulder.

"How fortunate," Mistress Tarsis said brightly, and stood to one side to speak while Master Tarsis signed his reply. She repeated: "Tomorrow, I shall have my maid return the compliment of your invitation with a selection of my favorite varieties. I delight in the discovery of new friendships as well as the opening of trade, and I would have you feel no less welcome than you have made us."

They bowed with their hands on their stomachs, but rose far more quickly than Lord Sans could respond, and so he was mid-rise as the Tarsises took their leave to enter the public courtyard. He flushed, but said no more, and the next group of guests passed by without comment.

Ibram watched one of the sailing lights drift out into the public courtyard. From the sounds of it, the party was going well, no screams or indelicate shouting. Maybe the Ruckus had worn itself out? That seemed a bit far-fetched, but apart from a few tripped servants and lost silverware, it all seemed to be working out. He chewed a corner of his mouth.

Lord Sans was trying to stretch his back without appearing to be stretching at all; it made him look a bit like a man rubbing up against a tree. Ibram looked away to hide his smile, and peered at the interior gate. One of the servants stationed out in the antechamber ducked inside; she walked quickly forward to the dais and dipped into a bow.

"Just one small party, my lord," she said. "And then the guards have told me the gates are closed."

Lord Sans nodded and cleared his throat. "Very well."

She stepped to one side. A brief swell of noise wafted in from outside and then fell silent. Ibram whipped both hands behind his back and stretched them behind him quickly, before letting them hang down at his thighs. A small pack of young lords—almost too young to be let out of their homes—

and their servants appeared at the mouth of the gate and then moved to either side, making way with deep bows that did nothing to make them look older. From their green and yellow tunics, it looked like they were Ealers from Lilibrite, the town down the road where the orchards of Lilia trees grew.

Lally glanced over at him, and Ibram shrugged to hide the sudden fizz in his blood. He tucked the curl of his smile between his teeth and leaned all his weight up onto his toes. He craned his neck and saw the twinkle of gold on a dark head. His stomach turned over as Lally pulled him back down on his heels just in time to watch Lady Azadiya make her entrance.

She stood half a head shorter than her companion, some Attendant from the sect, and smiled as she walked forward with her arms swinging freely. Her eyes still tilted up at the outer corners like someone had just told her a good joke; her shoulders were still broad and her chin sharp. Her dark hair was held back at the crown in a low braided bun, pierced with two small gold hair sticks to the right and one to the left, while the rest of her hair hung loose down her back in thick waves, so heavy it barely curled at the ends.

She passed by the house gift table with a polite smile and a quirk of her eyebrows. Ibram took a deep, slow breath. She was out of uniform, as usual. The Attendant wore the knee-length quilted green gambeson closed at the neck and side, the wrapped grey breeches, and tall leather boots. Lady Azadiya wore a satin green vee-necked dress, sleeveless, with a near translucent cream robe, topped by an overgown of gold lace that trailed to the ends of her fingertips and the soles of her boots, clasped by a wide leather belt itself closed by a braided rope. Trimstone drops twinkled in her ears, and three silver rings made personally by Ibram's father held pride of place on her right hand. Neither Lady Azadiya nor her Attendant carried a gar with them; it was a little funny to see them walk without hearing the accompanying thunk of their wooden staves. Ibram felt his smile slip free as he watched her walk to the front dais. The air turned heavy with her presence, as it always did, a feeling of pressure like the seconds before a storm.

Lally shook his elbow and he grunted. He wriggled himself free of her pinching grasp and stood apart. His heart pounded in his chest. He'd thought by changing the message Marshal Steward Pherick had dictated that she would be more likely to come to the party, but it did his confidence good to know his plan had actually worked.

"Lady Azadiya Hobon," her Attendant announced. "Fourth Mentor of the Preceptory of Yseult of the Sect of Seven Fires."

Ibram tilted his head; that voice sounded familiar. He squinted at the back of the young man's head. He was solidly built, with a thick neck and hands like shovels. His hair was dark and tightly curled, but worn almost shorn to his skull in the Southern style, so his ears stuck out a bit too abruptly from the sides of his head. He looked young enough to have been a Learner when Ibram had left Lityen, but he couldn't place him.

Lord Sans bowed deeply with his hands covering his stomach. Lady Azadiya extended her arms at her waist with her palms upward. As she curled her hands closed, Lord Sans rose.

"You honor my father's—my house, ladyship," Lord Sans said. He cleared his throat and smiled.

She ignored the slip. "And I very much enjoyed the surprise of the invitation," she said.

Lord Sans stepped down off the dais with Marshal Steward Pherick behind him. The light was dimming quickly. The Marshal Steward waved his left hand once at the gate, and the guards began to lower it by ropes on either side.

"Will you join me in the courtyard?" Lord Sans asked.

Her head tilted slightly. To show up side by side with her might be considered an implication of preference on Lady Azadiya's part. She coughed once and glanced behind her.

"I wouldn't wish to tear you away from the rest of your guests..." she said.

Lord Sans looked behind her and slowly flushed. He'd forgotten the group of young men who'd preceded her into the reception hall, and who were now awkwardly standing in what Ibram assumed was their own order of precedence, waiting to be welcomed.

"I shall go through, lordship," she said. "No party is complete without the host's grand entrance." She glanced over her shoulder and then waved her hand forward. "Ibram."

The room paused. Ibram's stomach turned over once more; he coughed and ducked his chin to his chest. Marshal Steward Pherick's mouth disappeared into a thin white line. Lady Azadiya turned her back and her Attendant fell in at her shoulder. Lally made a sound like a harp with its strings cut as Ibram stepped out from behind the house gift table, and followed Lady Azadiya into the public courtyard.

❧

A respectable distance from the entrance, Lady Azadiya paused and put her hands on her hips. She raised her chin to survey the interior gardens, where a crowd had gathered to watch Lady Sebbina as she admired the topiary, doubtless in the hope that she'd mumble something about the Imperial bureaucracy that could help their sixth aunt's first cousin get hired by the currency office. The pavilions were attracting quite a few curious drinkers, and the water clock had drawn an interested crowd as it flowed with...steaming purple water. Ibram winced. At least it was merely aesthetic?

"You promised me wine and a curse," Lady Azadiya said, looking at Ibram from the corner of her eye. "And where is your half-cloak?"

"We can start on the drinking portion immediately to your right, my lady," Ibram muttered. "And must you mention that so loudly?"

She laughed as she led the way further into the courtyard, and Ibram rubbed the back of his hand over his mouth. He eyed the troupe of circlers hired for the party. The vielle and citole players struck up a dancing tune, but no one seemed likely to take them up on it. The jugglers, also, were threatening to perform.

"Which part?" she asked over her shoulder, and Ibram diverted his attention. "And if you're not going to wear the entire outfit, then what happened to your brigandine? You are still his guardsmen, aren't you?"

Lady Azadiya stopped and turned around; her mouth pulled down into a considering frown. Ibram tugged down on the bottom of his gambeson, and a button loosened on his shoulder. He winced at it, the knot barely holding, and then tucked it under the flap. "I was never employed by him," he said.

"So you were brought back to Lityen in chains?" she asked.

He shook his head quickly. "No, ladyship," he said. "More of a go-between, really. Or a living travel compendium."

She hummed and looked about herself again. "It seems a strung together affair," she said, and waved her hand towards the garden.

Several other party guests, who clearly had decided to listen in, smothered their mouths and turned away. Lady Sebbina caught sight of them then; her mouth thinned in determination. A maid offered her something pink and steaming on a tray.

"Pray offer that to someone with an easeful stomach, girl," Lady Sebbina snapped loudly. "I have business elsewhere."

The maid withdrew, and another took her place, this time with a heavy tray of clear drinks. Lady Sebbina's cane thunked on the ground. Ibram licked his lips and shrugged.

"Lord Sans wanted a show of ease and comfort," he said, "less armor and more happy drinking."

Lady Azadiya took a step back into the crowd, and shook her head. "If he's got a curse on his hands, I see no reason for less security."

Ibram raised his hands. "Ladyship, please, he doesn't want anyone to know."

"Half of Lityen knew by lunch, mark me," she said, and began to move through the crowd again. "I had to beat off the offers of accompaniment with my gar."

Ibram rolled his eyes as he followed her. "I'm sure it's not such a great matter."

"Fix your button." Lady Azadiya laughed as she turned down the right-hand walkway. The public courtyard was, by tradition, the largest structure in a manor. At home, Ibram's family sold their best creations there to only select clientele, and in this at least the North was no different. Lord Sans had ordered that the entire length of the main courtyard be opened for his exhibition, so that all the guests mingled underneath the sealed glass canopy and trod over the garden in the middle or, supposedly, admired the flowing stream bisecting the far right side just before the smaller terraces.

"Has it only been little things? Buttons and steam and such like? Did we get you in trouble?" the Attendant asked. "Only Mentor said she wouldn't be able to greet you properly in the reception line."

"A bit more expensive than that," Ibram said. "Three batches of candies ruined because the fire roared without stoking. No one was hurt, but sugar costs, you know. Lost flatware, laundry to be redone...one of the kitchen boys collapsed a spit, and lost a day's dinner. A few of us who got near it have had some trying moments. I took a bit of a spill down some stairs, the steps broke underneath my feet!" The Attendant frowned, and Lady Azadiya looked at him sharply. Ibram chuckled. "I was fine. As for the other...it was only until the party, anyway."

"And now you're home!"

The Attendant grinned at him, a bright flash of teeth in his deeply tan skin. He seemed so familiar. Ibram felt himself squinting as if that would help bring the man's name into focus. The guests around them were mingling with one eye on the food and the other on their fellow partygoers. Someone's glass crashed to the ground and a scattering of laughter bubbled out; Ibram jerked his head towards the sound of the breakage.

A Kilk woman dressed in bright silks tied and wrapped around her entire body, head to toes, walked on her beribboned hands along the handrail next to them. Her feet waved high in the air. Lady Azadiya raised her eyebrows but said nothing as she led them to one of the small pavilions, where the servants had arranged small plates of slivered white cheese and dried redberries to go with the dainty cups of Halfrey ale. Here, they paused, and there was room enough for a proper greeting. Before Ibram could do more than place his hands on his stomach and duck into a partial bow, she had raised her palms up almost as if she was going to cup his face. He swallowed; he could feel the heat of her skin against his cheeks. She beamed at him, and he could hear the small crowd at the table fall briefly silent.

"*Ibram*," she said again. "Laumye the Blue has pointed you

home. Your letters failed to note you have grown taller, but no wider."

She laughed. He grinned as she curled her fingers back and dropped her hands down. Her clan bracelet slipped against her wrist, the carved beads of blue crystal and clear-flecked basalt, creamy bone and iridescent trimstone. Her palms and fingers were dyed a dark green, so she must have been at her research tables longer than she should have been.

"I put in everything else, just as you wished," he said. "That my height grew as I aged, I thought you would figure out for yourself."

She waved her hand. "Yes, yes, you were very good, but just because you are working as you go does not mean you are expected to run off and never come back."

"So Ama said," he replied. "But your contract was only for information you didn't have, and how am I supposed to know what minor detail you might find important? Better to have it all neatly arranged so you can sort through it at your leisure."

"Which of course I have in abundance."

Ibram ignored that as a grown man might. Behind him, he heard a yelp and a thud, like feet on wooden boards. He glanced behind him; the contortionist had fallen to the ground and was now scratching her covered head with her toes, as if puzzled. He turned back around. "If all plans came together, I would be on my way to the East to see if all those stories about the Valantin are true."

She sniffed. "Trust me, they never are."

The Attendant briefly covered his eyes in mortification, and Ibram noticed his hands as well as ladyship's were dyed green. He nodded and raised his right hand. "Is that why you were late, my lady?" he asked, and wiggled his fingers slightly.

The noise level in the little pavilion bobbled as they stood there. Ibram could feel eyes on him from all sides. The clasp holding his dagger to his belt loosened; he caught his hilt and reset the buckle.

"I was not late," she protested. "The reception hour had not finished, and if the hour hasn't finished then the timing of my arrival doesn't count."

"The wooly grass came in today," the Attendant added. "It needed to be prepared for the next round of combat trials."

"You were mashing up poultices in that?"

She shrugged and brushed her palms against each other. "Clothes wash."

"Still, I have to wonder what Lord Sans thought of it," Ibram said. "He's not met many Westerners, you know."

"I'm sure he found it a charming decorative addition to my outfit."

"He's probably going to ask why you never showed up to work with dyed hands, Master Ucalegon," the Attendant said, and knocked their shoulders together.

Ibram blinked and let him. "I...suppose not."

"Ibram," she said with a smile. "Do you not recognize Ahksell?"

Ibram felt his eyes widen. "No," he said, as a grin stretched his mouth. "Ahksell?"

"I told you he wouldn't remember," she said, and laughed.

The Attendant—*Ahksell Solari* of all the folk—smiled widely and spread his arms out. "I got taller," he said.

Ibram shook his head and grinned. "And broader and bigger and—and—"

When Ibram had left, Ahksell had been the scrawniest thirteen year old Learner, too small for his hands and feet. He'd been more often found up a glass apple tree than at his studies, and Ibram had been specially deputized by her ladyship to return Ahksell to the preceptory or keep him locked in his family orchard depending on the time of day. Now,

Ibram doubted there was a tree in the village Ahksell could climb without bending the trunk.

"And his voice broke," Lady Azadiya said, "To the delight of everyone who had to listen to him learn his third range of combat."

"*Mentor*," Ahksell whined, and Ibram laughed.

"All right, there's something familiar," he said. "But it's spring. What are you doing here?"

In the sects, education was split between the sexes. Boys were taught in summer and sent out to work in winter, and girls the reverse. It was as unchanging as the seasons themselves, and even the little town schools where the Preceptory of Bedris taught the unfortunate to read and number adhered to it.

Ahksell shrugged. "I came back early."

"Well, it's—it's good to see you," Ibram said.

"It's good to see you, too," Ahksell said. "It's not half so entertaining to get chased out of the orchard by your mother."

"Well, excitement keeps Ama young, so she says. Can you not buy your own glass apples now?"

"Where's the cheer in that?" Lady Azadiya asked. "Ahksell, two plates, yes?"

"Mentor," Ahksell said, and bowed before walking to the table where the crowd was slowly making inroads in the food and drink.

Ibram shook his head. "I can't have been away that long," he said.

"Five years brings a great deal of change," Lady Azadiya said.

He ducked his head slightly. "You haven't," he said.

She smiled but shrugged. It was true, though; she appeared as ageless as she had when he'd gone off. Alchemists tended to either age so slowly it made no matter to bother about it, or die too young to care. If Ibram had ever been forced to guess, he couldn't have put it more closely than that Lady Azadiya was somewhere in the garden of her thirtieth year and had been since they'd first met when he was all of ten.

Ahksell returned and handed her a small wooden cup of ale. He held a wooden charger of cheese and berries and a bowl of milk bun pudding—already half-eaten—above his left palm. Ibram raised his eyebrows. Ahksell's skills had improved since he'd been away. Lady Azadiya sipped once, wrinkled her nose, and handed the cup back. Ahksell offered her the small plate of snacks, complete with a golden two-pronged fork.

"The curse?" she prompted, and speared a piece of cheese. She popped it into her mouth, paused, and then set the little gold fork on the plate. She swallowed heavily.

"Mentor?" Ahksell asked.

"I'm going to assume some form of rot was included in the language?" she asked in a strangled voice. She cleared her throat. "Water, Ahk-la."

"Oh." Ahksell's eyes widened. He looked down at the plate and then back up to ladyship. "Yes, right back."

He rushed off, and Ibram turned his back to the garden and its denizens. Lady Azadiya coughed and put her hand to the bare skin below her collarbones. She grimaced.

"Sorry," Ibram said, and winced.

She swallowed a few more times and waved her hand at him, silently. "Was it a talisman?" she asked, and cleared her throat again.

"It was a cursebird," he replied. "Made out of rust and flower petals, I think. Flew about the family courtyard, dived at anyone who tried to catch it, and burst into bad-smelling smoke after demolishing the interior water clock."

"Yes, it does seem to have a problem with those," she muttered, looking across the courtyard.

Ibram turned around. He spotted a familiar lordly head darting through the pack towards the disturbance, trailed by the larger, more sedate form of the Marshal Steward. The water clock on the wall was pouring forth a mauve smoke, swirling in the air and hanging like fog. Several guests were waving their hands in front of their faces with servants armed with fans darting around them like a school of fish.

"Did you get close to it?" she asked.

"I saw it flying around the family courtyard," he said. "We all tried to catch it."

He glanced around him. It didn't seem like the guests closest to him were upset by the disturbance, but they were certainly beginning to crane their necks for a better view. Ibram felt his shoulders begin to hunch and forced them straight again. Beside him, Lady Azadiya was watching the running servants with a mildly amused expression. She lifted her hand as one of the maids began to trip on her hem and pushed her flattened palm forward by an inch. The maid recovered her balance and ran back into the frothing purple smoke with her woven fan raised for battle.

He sighed. "Oh no, ladyship," Ibram said loudly enough to be heard by the gathering spectators. "That is, actually, a Northern...belching clock. The water, you see, turns to smoke on the hour."

"How forward thinking," she said. Her mouth twitched decidedly before settling once more. "And we are all still using gravity. Ah, thank you."

Ibram glanced back. Ahksell had returned with the water in a heavy glass tumbler. Lady Azadiya took a healthy swig, and swallowed with a shudder. She stared out over the garden with widened eyes.

"Ahksell, this is sojin," she said with a faint cough.

"Well, it was water when the maid poured it for me."

"Impressive servants around here," she muttered, and took another sip.

Ahksell looked wide-eyed at Ibram and nodded towards the ongoing melee. Ibram shrugged, and Ahksell chuckled. He popped a spoonful of milk bun pudding into his mouth and licked his lips.

"Well, I say it serves them right," Ahksell said. "Seven months on the road back with a pack of snoops isn't what I call a pleasant journey."

He licked the honey off the back of his spoon. Ibram felt his eyebrows bow before his hairline, and took a quick look at the pavilion they'd just left. Most of the guests had begun to drift towards the next offering. Two servants now scurried away with a covered tray while another discreetly offered napkins. He stepped aside for another tray-bearing woman; she twisted to get through the crowd, and a small goblet wobbled off its perch. He bent down and thrust an arm out just as she went for it herself; they collided and the goblet smashed to the floor, splashing ale on Ibram's boots.

The serving woman jerked back with a gasp and collided with a guest, who bellowed like a boar with a sore tusk. She jumped out of the way, naturally, and Ibram watched in a kind of slow motion as the tray of drinks came toppling down on his position. He threw one arm up over his head, hunched in anticipation of a solid drenching, and then the tray—drinks almost tossed and all—froze in midair. The servant gave a little shriek and covered her mouth with both hands.

"Oh well caught, Ahksell," Lady Azadiya said. "That would have been quite a mess."

"Thank you, Mentor," Ahksell said, with strain in his voice. "Um, now..."

"Curl your fourth fingers inward and raise both hands, while sliding your left hand fingers-forward. And get up,

Ibram, you look silly down there. Take the tray again, mistress. It's fine, you're not in any trouble."

He heard the servant make a sound that reminded him dimly of assent, and figured that was as good as he was going to get from a Northerner. A local wouldn't have been so mealy over a bit of physical alchemy. Slowly, Ibram rose as the tray veered away from the space over his head. He pulled down his gambeson, cleared his throat, and frowned. His boot was damp, and now he'd have to spend the rest of the day smelling of ale.

Ahksell had his hands outstretched: his left, palm up, was further than his right, palm-down. He had bitten his bottom lip bloodless, and breathed heavily through his wide nose. His eyes lay on the tray wobbling a bit in the air, but then he flicked them up to the servant, and grinned tensely. "Do you have hold of the tray, mistress?"

She winced as she grabbed the tray with both hands. "Yes, master," she said grimly. It bobbled in her grip but the drinks stayed upright this time. She flung herself back into the pavilion, and Ibram turned away.

Lady Azadiya laughed lightly as Ahksell let his arms fall to his sides and took a deep breath. Ibram caught Ahksell's eye and nodded in relief. The crowd buzzed mildly with approval, but soon returned to their conversations.

"Exciting," Lady Azadiya said. "And very well done, Ahksell." She looked over Ibram's shoulder and then refocused on him. "Not too wet, I hope?"

Ibram shook his head. "Just my boot. Thanks to Ahksell."

Ahksell shook his head. "A lucky catch," he said. "I'm still learning."

Lady Azadiya was watching something from far off, but turned her head at that. "Believe in luck on your own time, Ahk-la," she said. "My Attendants never need it."

Ahksell rubbed one hand over his cheek and grinned. "No, Mentor."

Ibram thought he heard a familiar thump on the walkway, rigorously regular and followed by stiff footsteps. He cocked his head to the left and back.

"Now, this cursebird," her ladyship said briskly. "Did it enter any of the other courtyards?"

Ibram turned back around. "Just the family's and the servants'—"

"Show me at once!" she declared.

She swept right, down the lacquered wooden pathway that led towards the next pavilion, and further on to the smaller gardens. Ibram found himself once again dragged along in her current with Ahksell beside him.

"Lady Sebbina's coming and our Lord Preceptor hasn't been to a council meeting in months," Ahksell whispered.

Ibram coughed into his shoulder to hide his grin. He chanced a quick look back over his shoulder, and caught Lady Sebbina's sharp eyes just before she was obscured by a group of obsequious contract men in Tyal blue. Their loud, oily eloquence diverted the ladyship's march, and Ibram turned back around with a shudder. He was only obeying a guest, after all.

"What does she want with Lady Azadiya anyway?" he whispered to Ahksell.

Ahead, he saw Lady Azadiya's head twitch. Ahksell shrugged next to him. "I think it's more that Mentor's the closest one who's deigned to come down the living mountain," he said. "And since none of them will come down, then Lady Sebbina most certainly cannot come up."

Ibram snorted. Diplomacy and politics had never been his study, but he could grasp the edges of it enough to know the tricks were mostly down to posturing and foolishness. Though, to be sure, now that he was back in Lityen, the terms of the bargain he'd made with Ama and Father had to be upheld. If the Sect of Seven Fires still wished to employ him, as it employed almost everyone else in his family, then he was its agent. And if he was its agent, then he would no doubt be seconded to Lady Azadiya's staff, just as Ama had been. Best to know the general feeling of the sect in which he would be working.

"What keeps the rest of you penned up?" he asked.

Ahksell waggled his head from left to right. "Most of the rest of us are too busy getting ready for the Festival, you know. The Preceptory of Afsoun blew up their training ground to make way for a pond! There's a rumor that they're going to stage a recreation of the first, uh, pumping, as it were."

"They're going to recreate a sewage system," Ibram said.

Ahskell nodded. "That's the common thought, yes."

"Not with *actual* sewage, though?"

Ahksell rocked his head left and right and then shrugged. "Probably not," he answered slowly. "But it would be a pity if it were just water, after all."

"Wine?" Ibram suggested.

"The First Mentor of Afsoun drinks nothing but shay," Lady Azadiya said. "At best, we can hope for sweet cider, and probably at room temperature."

Ahksell chuckled and nodded his head. Ibram gagged slightly, but recovered himself. Cider was his preferred drink, but even first rate cider was cloying when it was warm.

The crowd parted for Lady Azadiya without even seeming to realize it, readjusting themselves to one side or the other in the middle of conversations or even eating, and then coming together again with barely a blink. He saw the Tarsises watching their little group from across the garden.

"I've heard a rumor that Lord Sans has something special planned for the party," Ahksell said.

Ibram nodded. "He's got a lot of ideas, or, well, he likes the idea of ideas."

"How philosophical of him," Ahksell replied. "Just like the Sect Above The Clouds."

"More like he enjoys changing his mind."

"Don't we all?" Lady Azadiya asked.

Ibram lowered his voice. "Not when we're half-way down a mountain, six miles from the nearest bed, and someone wants to 'experience the balmy air.'"

Ahksell laughed. Across the way, Ibram could see the regular guardsmen in their stations, posted at relatively inconspicuous points along the walkways. The sky behind the sealed glass roof had darkened. Lally was using one of the long, leaf-shaped fans to stir the air above the fountain and send a moored cluster of light ships back out to illuminate the rest of the party. Ibram breathed in and smelled the beeswax candles as they sailed forth.

The jugglers had placed themselves out on the lawn and were tossing sticks in the air. Four stubby painted clubs flew end over end in a dizzying pattern. The closest juggler drew a fifth one from his belt and let fly. Ahksell watched them with wide eyes. "In light of all the—the *business*," he said in what Ibram assumed Ahksell believed was an intimate voice, the approximate volume of a bullroarer. He raised his hands to quiet him, but Ahksell continued. "Is it wise of Lord Sans to have all these—these Kilk folks about?"

Ladyship shook her head. "It's only the bendable one."

"The circlers are perfectly professional, I'm certain," Ibram said. "Even if they might—" One of the jugglers dropped a stick and kicked it up high in the air for his partner to catch; it arched over the other man's feathered hat and disappeared into the crowd. A startled yelp erupted; a crowd of young ladies clapped. "They should be fine."

Ibram rubbed his eyebrow with his thumbnail. Ahksell shook his head.

⁂

"Does Lord Sans take great care of his wine?" Lady Azadiya asked, and swished a mouthful of yellow-green tolnic behind her lips. They had rather neatly escaped the encroaching rot by ordering directly from the servants, a process that took longer than picking up items from the tables, but resulted in someone else noticing a spoiled drink before it reached her ladyship's mouth. She swallowed. "Well, under normal circumstances."

Ibram glanced around. They were in a small bubble of space; most of the guests had formed a bit of a line for the pavilion with the resin wine tasting. One of the contractmen —dressed with a silverback fish badge, so Vo Goran, perhaps? —had a notebook in hand as he watched Lady Azadiya from the corner of his eye. The Fourth Mentor's wine choice was a point of interest for any discerning political mind in Lityen, even when the chance of her favor was slim to none. Their eyes met briefly, and the contractman glanced away with a sniff. Ibram had forgotten the way the crowds reacted to them, the way most strangers eyed him as if they couldn't figure out what he was doing by their side. He had no talent for alchemy, and nothing to recommend him but his own hands. He chewed the corner of his mouth.

He shook his head and put it out of his mind; her ladyship was waiting for her answer. "He drinks enough of it, but I don't think he could tell you which end of the barrel had the spigot," Ibram said. "Was the ale truly foul?"

"As ales go, I am no judge," she said. Beyond her shoulder, Ibram saw certain others make a note. "But the cheese was definitely off. As was the melon in syrup, unfortunately."

Ibram winced. "My apologies, my lady."

"He doesn't sell cheese or fruit, fortunately." She shook her head dismissively and glanced at him. The corners of her eyes crinkled when she smiled. "Was it your fault?"

"Perhaps it was just the journey," Ahksell said. "It's hard to tell with cheeses. After all, they all smell terrible."

Ibram laughed and ducked his head while Ahksell grinned at him. He picked up the pace a little; his steps felt lighter than usual. They strolled along the edge of the garden, and Ibram watched one of the guests pick a blossom off a calendula and hand it to her maid.

"What did the cursebird say, Ibram?" Lady Azadiya asked.

"Hm? Oh." Ibram refocused. He tucked his hand around the hilt of his dagger. "It screamed mostly."

"It screamed?" she repeated, and raised one eyebrow.

They moved aside for a passing servant with a tray loaded with milk buns and honey. Ibram smoothed his hands down his gambeson and watched it pass carefully.

"Very loudly," he said finally. "I think it shattered the morning tea set."

"And that was all?"

Ibram shook his head. "No, it said..." He cleared his throat and ducked his head, which put him at the height of her shoulder. She smelled like...something sugary. He stepped back quickly, and saw Ahksell eating a new milk bun slowly drowning in a bowl of honey with a spoon. He lowered his voice instead. "It said 'Go back or make diamonds from snow! Stay and rot your house! Go back!' and then it blew up."

"A short message," she said.

"Very pointed," Ahksell poked the air with his spoon.

"Make diamonds from snow?" Lady Azadiya muttered. "What's that about?"

"It's something they say up there," Ibram said, and

shrugged. "You know, make diamonds from snow, carve your name into the river, farm your beans from rocks, shove—"

"Yes, thank you, I understand the reference," she interrupted. She set her cup on the railing; her hair swayed as she shook her head. "It's harmless, I suppose," she said. "But how did it get in?"

"Ah, Lady Azadiya!" Lord Sans called out. "There you are!"

Yilka's *megrims*. Ibram barely managed to stifle his groan. All three of them turned to watch as Lord Sans, trailed by Marshal Steward Pherick, made his way over to where they stood. Ibram retreated to a more respectable distance and tucked his hand around his hilt. The leather wrapping rubbed against his fingers. His stomach bubbled.

Lord Sans bounded up to the middle step of the small stairs that led out of the sunken garden and bowed slightly, having already been introduced. "I hope you've been enjoying the party so far, ladyship," he said.

"A lovely occasion, Lord Sans," she said.

Lord Sans' head bobbed in agreement. "You grace my courtyard, ladyship." He clasped his hands behind his back and puffed up his chest just like a cave sparrow. Behind his shoulder, Marshal Steward Pherick smiled faintly. He had a good business face, but Ibram noted that his eyes were never still, constantly looking past the group to check on what was happening around the public courtyard.

"Is there a libation you particularly enjoyed, ladyship?" Lord Sans asked. "I could make a note of it and have a portion decanted for you to take back to your preceptory..."

Lady Azadiya's face was perfectly placid. "I thank you for the thought, but I haven't made a full circuit of the courtyard yet. I will, of course, remember such a kind offer."

"Ah, well..." Here Lord Sans trailed off in thought. Ibram supposed Yilka the Green held fools' tongues when they couldn't do it themselves. The young lord had had many smart ideas about how to manage old barbarian ladies on the caravan road down, but none of the choice bits Ibram remembered seemed to be in evidence now. He had more red in his face than confidence.

"But there is still time yet!" Lord Sans finally declared, a little too loudly, which caused Lady Azadiya to rock briefly back on her heels. "Perhaps Ucalegon here can be persuaded to tell you his favorites. Act as a sort of guide, you see."

Lady Azadiya nodded slowly. "On that, Ibram might. He was so long in the world, his family feared they might never see him again."

"But here he is! And he had good judgement, too. Why, we would never have made it here if not for him!" Lord Sans exclaimed.

"Truly?" Lady Azadiya asked mildly.

"We must thank the Imperial postmaster," Lord Sans said. "His poor eyesight was a boon to everyone concerned, don't you think, Ladyship?"

Ibram held his breath, and even Marshal Steward Pherick noticeably winced. Lady Azadiya tilted her head ever so slightly. A small silence developed; Lord Sans went a little green about the mouth.

Lord Halfrey's officially polite fiction for locking Ibram up had been the 'mistake' at the small Imperial Scribes' Bureau in Halfrilat. Somehow, Ibram had neglected to seal his letters correctly. In the spirit of that duty owed to each and every subject of the Vissilian Empire, the Imperial Postmaster had read Ibram's mail, rather than simply the address tag on the cord, and enlisted his lord's aid in finding Ibram to return the letter to its writer. In gratitude, Ibram had promised Lord Halfrey's son an introduction.

In reality, an aged cousin from a cadet Halfrey branch had heard Ibram mention Lady Azadiya's name in a draughtshop. Nothing impolite, of course, merely that he was in correspondence with her. Though it hadn't done much to impress the potgirl, said Aged Cousin had declined to believe an arm-for-hire traveling alone would be in contact with anyone of noble birth unless it was for one of those occasionally heated altercations between noble houses. They'd gone through his belongings like a hot knife through jam. Ibram didn't normally think of himself as an eloquent speaker, but he'd leave rose cake to Yilka the Green for the next fifty years in recompense for the tale he'd spun his freedom out of in Halfrilat. It all ended well enough, of course.

Ahksell cleared his throat. "Lordship, may I ask, how did you bring so many casks down from your family's manor? I heard there was even an ice wine on offer, but how could you carry it south so far without it spoiling?"

Lord Sans latched onto Ahksell's question with a brilliantly relieved smile. He squared his shoulders and leaned to the left as if he could escape Lady Azadiya's regard.

"The alchemists, of course!" he cried. His eyes widened a bit; Ahksell was broad enough to be two of the young lord. "These casks were commissioned especially for our journey from the Sect Above the Clouds. They've been created with a special talisman inside that keeps the contents unchanged."

"Truly?" Ahksell asked. "That is a marvel, lordship. Do you have an open example? Would it be too much to see it?"

"Oh, I..." Lord Sans paused and bit his lower lip. He glanced about his company and then back to the Marshal Steward, before visibly reminding himself that he was in charge. "Well, it couldn't hurt anything. Attendant, uh—"

Ibram looked at Marshal Steward Pherick, who was observing his master. As an Attendant of a great sect, Ahksell's standing was perfectly sufficient to speak with a noble of Lord Sans' minor house, but since the sects themselves were a hotbed of the great and small, folk were often confused about the status of sect members upon being introduced. Perhaps for once in his life, Lord Sans would choose caution and not condescend to someone on first meeting?

"Solari, lordship," Ahksell said. He smiled. They were of an age, weren't they? Ibram blinked and chuckled a little to himself. How odd to think of it.

"Attendant Solari, it would be no trouble to show you one of the casks," Lord Sans said in a rush. "I believe we had one opened for the winter Pyrus cider in the pavilion over the bridge. May I—come with me, and I will show you."

Ahksell turned to Lady Azadiya, who had been watching them with a faintly amused eye. "Mentor?" he asked.

She waved her hand in the direction of the garden. "Away with you," she said. "Bring back knowledge."

"Can I..." Ahksell held out his bowl, still filled at the bottom with a pool of honey, and Ibram took it. The spoon clattered from his grip and tumbled down the length of Ibram's trouser leg, leaving a shining, sticky trail like a slug smear down the wool. Ibram breathed out through his nose and bent to pick up the spoon. He set it back in the bowl and left the whole mess on the ground, wiping his fingers on the side of the walkway.

Ahksell bowed to her and turned to Lord Sans. "Then I will be pleased to see it," he said. He dipped his upper body forward.

Lord Sans swallowed and nodded. He stepped back into Marshal Steward Pherick, then returned to his original step; a thin red blotch bloomed upon his cheeks as he moved to one side and abandoned the stairs for the garden floor. Ibram moved aside so Ahksell could join the young lord. Lord Sans had to crane his neck upwards to make eye contact as he led Ahksell across the grass, already deep in explaining the merits of winter Pyrus over the summer varieties.

They watched the pair walk away. Marshal Steward Pherick cleared his throat politely.

"A fine student, ladyship," he said. "With your permission, I shall withd—"

Lady Azadiya turned to him. "Indeed so," she replied. "And you, Marshal Steward Pherick? Are you enjoying Lityen?"

The Marshal Steward paused; he wasn't, as far as Ibram could gather, a man for long conversations. As a Marshal Steward he was used to conversing in public with nobility, to be certain, but apart from endlessly repeating the family histories of those nobles Lord Sans had met along the way, Ibram could count on one hand the number of conversations in which Marshal Steward Pherick had willingly taken part. Lady Azadiya had him by the manners, though; it wasn't like he could refuse to speak on the grounds of propriety. He shifted his weight on the garden step. "We have perhaps of late had a flutter of trouble."

Lady Azadiya nodded. "Just so? Well, that's the valleys for you. Once you get to a mere 200 miles above sea level, there's really nothing to do but stir up a fight. What have you chosen?"

He chuckled stiffly. "Ladyship, I cede to your experience on the matter, but I fear I've no time to make my own trouble."

Lady Azadiya resettled the fall of her left sleeve and smoothed the fabric between her fingers. Her upturned eyes gleamed slightly. "As you say, Marshal Steward," she said. "Tell me, how do you like your new home?"

"I fear I have never been so far down from the North before," he said. "The heat does affect me, but the need to set up the household for my lord has occupied a great deal of my focus. I look forward to learning more when there's a bit more time."

"You're to take over the running of the household, then?" she asked.

Marshal Steward Pherick nodded. Ibram narrowed his eyes. The Marshal Steward wasn't moving, but he seemed… shorter? He glanced around, but no one else seemed to notice anything.

"Lord Halfrey has provided funds to purchase a manor should all go well." Marshal Steward Pherick flicked his eyes briefly to Ibram. "I suppose it all depends on the company my lord gathers to him now."

"Oh, there's plenty of young lords in the province," she said, and tilted her head. Her hair swung against her back. "I sometimes think they grow them alongside the trees. Is it a Northern custom to—Marshal Steward, you appear to be sinking."

"I—oh my small gods!" Marshal Steward Pherick's breath choked in his throat as he looked down. Ibram stepped forward and craned his neck. The garden stairs were sinking into the ground as if it was quicksand, a puddle of grass and gravel spreading like waves in a pond. The Marshal Steward's arms flew out to the side as he wobbled backwards. Lady Azadiya flung her arm out; she crooked the first two fingers of her right hand and the Marshal Steward froze, tilted in mid-air, with his eyes bugging out of his face and his mouth agape like the fish.

"His arm, Ibram," she said quickly, and Ibram shook himself all over.

He reached out, grabbed Marshal Steward Pherick with both hands, and towed him upright. It felt like tugging an empty sack—just enough drag to know he held something, but no real weight behind it. Ibram stepped backwards to make room on the walkway for Marshal Steward Pherick and then released him. He ducked his head, took another step back, and swallowed.

"Are you all right, sir?" he asked.

"I…yes, I'm…" Pherick breathed in deeply and smoothed

both hands down either side of his gambeson. He shook his head and raised his chin. "Yes, I'm very well, thank you."

A small whispering crowd had gathered, but the Marshal Steward ignored them, so Ibram did as well. They both turned to Lady Azadiya, who was standing at the edge of the walkway with her arm outstretched and her palm down, an arrow-shaped pendant of banded rock on a braided copper and silver chain hung from her fingers. The stone at first hung motionless and then began to make a slow, clockwise circle. Ibram winced. Below them, the garden stairs had fully sunk to the top level, now surrounded by solid looking ground. It wasn't a very long drop—no more than one and a half feet at most—but everyone had seen it. He could hear an excited murmur amongst the crowded guests, and Master Tarsis was signing something apparently quite amusing to his assembled group. Ibram gently rearranged his gambeson; his brigandine coat would have been far more reassuring right then.

"No harm done," Lady Azadiya announced. She snapped the pendant back into her palm. Ibram tore his attention away from the ground. "My dear Marshal Steward, I'm afraid you've been the victim of damp."

"Damp?" Marshal Steward Pherick echoed. His face was pale and splotched with red.

"Oh yes," she said, and turned to him. "We're constantly having to replace wooden stairs around here, you know. It gets very wet in the valleys, and once the wood has swollen there's no going back."

She smiled and folded her hands, the picture of calm. The pendant had disappeared, of course, probably up her sleeve. She continued to smile in the face of the guests, until around them the crowd slowly began to mutter to itself about how that was true, wasn't it? Hadn't cousin Lalten taken a fall just like that after a hard rain, and oh his mother had been so angry, it ruined his best tunic. No accounting for old wood, and the Vo Messyn were never very conscientious on maintenance, and so on and so on, until they began to disperse, only a little disappointed in their brush with theater.

Ibram looked up at the clear glass canopy above them and cleared his throat. Belatedly, Marshal Steward Pherick put his hands on his stomach and bowed. He still seemed a little pale.

"Thank you, ladyship," he said as he stood back up again. "I didn't—I would hate..."

She waved her hand. "Nothing to it," she said. "Your little trouble, I imagine?"

Marshal Steward Pherick froze except for the thinning line of his mouth. Having been ordered not to speak of the Ruckus to strangers, he couldn't agree, of course, but the slow thawing of his shoulders seemed to be enough acknowledgment for her ladyship. Ibram licked his lips and tucked his hands behind his back.

Lady Azadiya hummed to herself and turned in a slow circle. She surveyed the main courtyard and its smoking purple water clock and the milling crowds of Lord Sans' potential clientele. Her skirts belled out a little and then settled as she came back around to face them.

"I must say this is an interesting party," she said. "Do you know, I see nothing out of the ordinary at all?"

Ibram stepped briefly to the side to make way for a small collection of young lords and ladies, each carrying wine glasses in both hands and trailing a straggling gaggle of servants. He turned back to her ladyship in time to see her pinch the hem of her sleeve and tug it further over her hand. A small shriek erupted behind him, but he saw one of the other Northerners running up the garden path and so ignored it.

"Ladyship?" Marshal Steward Pherick asked.

She smiled. "I'm of the Preceptory of Yseult, you know. Our study is the physical body."

"Yes," he said. "I...thought it was something medical?"

She laughed, and there was a discernible ripple in the group of youngsters daring each other to approach the stairs in the garden. "Oh no," she said. "We're not a university, after all, we're alchemists. We refine and perfect the world around us, not merely argue over its contents. No, everything in the world is composed of a physical body, Marshal Steward, you, me, the grass, the steps, the air we breathe. To understand ourselves is to understand our sphere of reality. And once you are in control of that, you may affect every body as well. So your curse—"

"Ladyship," Marshal Steward Pherick murmured.

She waved her hand. "I find it interesting," she said, obligingly lowering her voice, "that I see nothing in this courtyard that does not belong to the physical world, nothing either demonic or divine. The steps and the ground resonate just as they should."

Marshal Steward Pherick paused. "I'm afraid, ladyship," he said finally, "that I don't follow your meaning."

She smiled, and Ibram briefly squeezed his eyes shut in preparatory despair. "Why, it means much," she said. "It means this is no curse, but a cantrip, and that's *far* more interesting—and to be truthful, far better for you in the long run."

"But there was a cursebird," Marshal Steward Pherick protested, and then flinched. He lowered his voice. "The family courtyard is ruined."

"The new Lord Vo Messyn is going to take this cleaning bill out of your hide, I fear. They're very attached to this place."

The new Lord Vo Messyn, as Ibram remembered, had been renting his manor from a townhouse in Sobrilat for the last forty years. He supposed he was fond of the place, as luxury did cost. "And it was loud as a wounded bumple," Ibram added. "Just as high-pitched, too."

"Such a smart boy," she said. "Clever and sharp as your mother. Nevertheless, it's not a curse. There's very few people here who could muster the belief or the anger for one anyway. It's a mark in your favor."

"I don't follow," Marshal Steward Pherick said faintly.

"Well, if it was a curse, you'd have to find out why your household gods let it slip through—I find a lack of good drink is usually the cause—but if it's simply a cantrip, then anyone of particular outrage could have bought an automaton and set it to flying." She smiled. "Usually that's far less expensive and, considering the bird disintegrated, it shouldn't be more than a week or two of upset. Curses are far more insidious. Think of the boils, Marshal Steward! You could have been covered in them. Or... what did it say, Ibram? Snow in the garden? Awful, I'm sure."

Marshal Steward Pherick didn't look much less upset. A fine dew had settled on his temples. "We did leave several offerings at Lord Sans' personal shrine," he said. "And they were well received."

Lady Azadiya nodded encouragingly.

"It is...also true that the incidents haven't stopped," Marshal Steward Pherick said. "We tried a cone of camber root incense?"

She spread her hands in front of her, and Marshal Steward Pherick sighed deeply.

"But what will happen?" he asked.

"Oh, they go away on their own," her ladyship said. "The weak ones do, anyway, and I see no signs that it's a strong cantrip. It's rather..."

She caught Ibram's eye and held it for a short moment that still made him catch his breath behind his teeth. She looked away, quick as a bird, and surveyed the courtyard again. Lady Azadiya had a mind that cornered three rogue conundrums at breakfast and forced them to terms by supper, but Ibram could remember at least sixty dinners where her appearance at the table was in body only.

Marshal Steward Pherick cleared his throat and raised his eyebrows. He pointed to her ladyship and spread his hands. Ibram shrugged and supplied what he hoped was a soothing expression on his face. The Marshal Steward cleared his throat again.

A short silence developed. Lady Azadiya plucked a delicate stemmed glass from a servant passing below her and several feet away. Marshal Steward Pherick turned a dull pink; none of these Northerners seemed to know how to behave with alchemists. She took a small, careful sip, as it was filled to the brim with a viscous liquid so blue it was almost purple.

"Trembleberry wine," she said. She held the glass in front of her. "An old favorite. How did you get it to grow out of the mountains?"

"Ladyship, mountains have been found even in the North." Marshal Steward Pherick took a breath that puffed his chest out and then deflated. He bowed slightly and spoke without meeting her ladyship's eyes. "Ladyship," he said. "Would it be—?"

Ibram heard the sudden sound of footsteps and the decided stump of a walking stick on wooden boards. Oh, *hang*. He glanced at Lady Azadiya.

"Not to fret," she said brightly, already walking backward across the short bridge. "Ibram will show me the inner apartments. What a wonderful idea, Marshal Steward! I love this drink, Ibram, come along and find me another cup."

Ibram winced and raised his hands in a helpless gesture as he brushed past Marshal Steward Pherick, who watched him go with a look of increasing perturbation cracking the glaze of his composure. Ibram jerked his head to the right, and the Marshal Steward spun just in time to bow.

"Lady Sebbina!" he cried as Ibram quick-stepped down the walkway.

Lady Azadiya had reached the end of the bridge and stepped onto the next platform with a determined stride that had the crowd parting for her like she was a scythe and they were tall grass. A passing sailing light trailed in her wake. Ibram caught up to her five feet from the doorway to the family courtyard and for his trouble was smacked in the face by a rogue lock of hair wafting in the breeze.

"I will not be pinned down by a bureaucrat," Lady Azadiya muttered to herself. "I'm the Fourth Mentor, I don't have to talk to the Empire if I don't want to, and that's why we have— what have we here?"

A crowd of heavyset servants swayed out from the far doors, carrying the large cask and frame constructed to preserve the ice wine. Ibram felt his shoulders draw tight with tension at their approach. They stumped forward, hands white-knuckled around the gigantic frosted frame, and the entire crowd gave way before their sweating faces.

Lady Azadiya hopped up to sit on the railing as Ibram and the rest of the crowd pressed themselves to either side. She watched the cask pass by and eyed the swaying cooling charms lined within its frame. Somewhere behind Ibram's back, the musicians struck up a fanfare that followed the servants as they lurched to wherever they'd finally decided to show off Lord Sans' most expensive commodity.

"Oh, Ibram, there you are," she said, once the crowds began following the cask. "Come and open this door for me."

She waved her empty wine glass at the closed door and the guardsman—Zevin, from the Northern lowland—braced in front of it. The guardsman looked Ibram and raised both pale eyebrows.

"Zevin, I'm supposed to show ladyship the family garden," he said. "She...likes honey lamps."

"I press them in books," Lady Azadiya said. "Here."

She tossed the rest of the wine down her throat and handed her glass to Zevin; he took it and then twisted the center latch, staring at her ladyship all the while. Lady Azadiya licked a stray drop from the corner of her mouth. Zevin clasped the glass to his chest one-handed but held the door open admirably as she wafted past him.

"You can close it after us," Ibram said as he passed.

"Should I lock it, too?" Zevin asked.

"What good would that do?"

The door thudded shut, and the lock definitely turned. A pair of servants loitering with empty trays by the opposite door looked up at the noise and then returned to their gossip. Ibram blinked at the sudden muffling of party noise; the silence charms worked into the lintel were still functioning, at least.

"Who the cangsa has been shearing these bushes?" Lady Azadiya called out. She was staring out at the garden from one of the stairs leading down to it. The stains and smoke damage seemed a little worse now that she was looking at them. "It looks like someone burst a pressure vessel in here."

"No, just a cursebird."

She turned back to him, smiled, and raised one finger. "Ah, not a cursebird, Ib-la. A cantrip vessel."

"I hate it when you call me that," he said as he walked forward. The servants at the far end were unsuccessfully pretending not to pay attention.

She stepped down into the denuded garden and walked to the fountain. "It's a term of affection."

"It makes me sound like a phosphate drink."

Lady Azadiya laughed and then frowned down into the ruined bowl of the fountain. "Why is there bread in here?"

Ibram sighed and jogged forward to join her. "Does it matter? The Ruckus did all this."

He rotated his left hand in a circle in the air, and she waggled her head from side to side. She rubbed two fingers against the red stain on the lip of the fountain and then frowned down at her fingertips. She licked them, and Ibram groaned.

"I forgot you did that," he said. "What possible use is it?"

Lady Azadiya spit to the side. "You can make this argument when you haven't faced an army of the demonic undead that turned out to be a mercenary band with access to a timoleon bog."

"Well, you sure licked them." She flicked her fingers at him and Ibram winced at the invisible plonk to the head. He rubbed the spot with the heel of his palm and grinned. "Is that where we get the expression from?"

"I am not that old," she said. She turned and waved at the servants, who straightened up with startled faces. "Can I be given a glass of aired?" She turned around. "Do they have aired here?" She turned back. "If not, then a nice shay, hmm? Strain the leaves."

The servants looked from her ladyship to Ibram and back again.

"Nothing for me, thank you," he said.

They disappeared into the kitchens with bobbed bows. Lady Azadiya tucked her hair over her right shoulder. "The Ruckus, hmm?"

He shrugged. "What else to call it?"

She looked up at the glass canopy. "No, it's adorable. I'm always impressed by your way with descriptions."

He snorted. When she wasn't in company, her ladyship's western accent came rolling back, lilting like water over rocks. "Maybe I wouldn't be here if you were less impressed."

"That was not the bargain you struck with your family," she said. "You were always to come back."

She looked over the courtyard with a slight frown. The stains were still there, of course, but they'd cleaned up the splinters from the broken railing and removed the beams. The grass looked only the smallest bit crispy, and apart from the acrid smells clinging to every surface, it didn't look so awful, really. Certainly nothing to worry about when the Vo Messyn returned to their manor.

"By way of the eastern grasses, sure enough," he said. "Not the quickstep tumble from Halfrilat trailing a young lord and his mobile wine shop because—"

She put her hands on her hips. "Because people who steal other people's mail often don't enjoy what they wind up reading. Which is really their own fault, when you think about it."

"Possibly they didn't enjoy my selection of hand drawn maps, ladyship."

She sniffed. "Then they should build better homes," she declared, deliberately missing the point. "I don't suppose you made copies before they destroyed them?"

Ibram shrugged. "No, ladyship, my apologies. Paper was expensive on the road, and as you say, I have a way with words."

She tilted her head with a smile and tilted her head. "Well, it was much appreciated, no matter how curtailed."

He huffed a chuckle.

"I suppose that's why the Halfrey brought their wares this far from their lands," she said.

He inhaled and nodded. "I think so, yes. Lityen by itself is too small, but—"

"There lay an entire sect of alchemists, stuck up the living mountain with broad tastes and so little to spend their money on, even with the inland port, and an arm-for-hire with an introduction hovering about his lips," she finished.

"I wouldn't call it 'hovering,' really. In my travel pouch?"

She snorted. "What a feast for the pocketbook."

"I don't know why they wouldn't think you would be angry," he said, and shook his head. "I still don't know, really. They aren't paying you, after all."

She raised her eyebrow briefly. "Money to small houses comes only following the seizing of an opportunity," she said. "How many children does Lord Halfrey have again?"

"Ten," he said. "Half and half again."

She spread her stained palms and shrugged. "Just so," she said. "And money to be made as well? A connection to the garden provinces of Vissilia? Come now, you've been traveling far enough to guess Lord Halfrey's thought."

He waggled his head from side to side and rolled his eyes. "Suppose so, my lady," he said, and only twisted his lips down for a moment. "Ruined the plan, though."

"Really more of an outline," she said.

"And I still don't know why you couldn't do it yourself."

She groaned. "So much paperwork, Ibram," she said. "When I leave the mountain there are rules and signatures and—"

"Escorts and duties and *parties*," they finished together.

"I was almost chained for a spy, you know," he said. "They thought I wanted inside their distilleries."

"But when a young man gives me the state of the roads and villages, full of his freedom..." she continued as if she hadn't heard, and Ibram laughed. She continued. "You're very sharp. You could write a book! Handy for travelers everywhere."

"I was trying to make my way in the world."

"And *this* way you made your way into an inn, rather than resting in a ditch; it really isn't as fun as you think it will be."

Not much argument there, although it could also be said that he'd still wound up his nights in a few ditches anyway.

Purely by chance, near towns with friendly draughtshops, of course. The loose button on his gambeson had worked itself free again; he tucked it back. He shrugged and she copied him and then crossed her arms across her chest. She whirled in a circle and then came down hard on her heels.

"The canopy can open?" she asked.

"No, I don't think so."

"But the courtyards were opened for airing?"

He shook his head. "Just the family and servants' areas. The thing flew around our heads, shrieking."

"The Vo Messyn were wealthy, but not ostentatious. Is the servant courtyard open air?"

He nodded. "Yes, the cursebird—"

"Cantrip vessel."

"The *automaton* erupted in the family courtyard."

"But it could have flown in through the servants' area."

"One of the guardsmen would have seen it," Ibram said. "Or one of the servants. They don't know anything, and believe me, they were questioned. The head cook can spot a worm in a melon at fifty paces, I swear."

"The Wheelmaker makes his own luck," she muttered. She reached into her left sleeve and pulled out her pendant pendulum again. She hung the chain from the second knuckle of her middle right finger and watched it sway. The arrow-shaped rock swung in lazy arcs before hanging at an angle towards the fountain.

"The bird did explode here," Ibram said.

Lady Azadiya hummed in her throat and snapped the pendulum back into her palm. She hitched up her skirts and stepped up into the fountain. Ibram looked around him quickly.

"My—get down from there, you'll get bread in your boots."

She laughed and pulled herself up by the middle bowl to

peer into the smallest on top. "Someone has a ready arm, there's bread in here, too! You're going to get ants. And...ooh, hello lovely."

Giggles erupted from the servants' doorway. He looked over, frowning, and saw one of the girls from before slowly approaching with a small silver tray and a steaming fluted glass cup. He looked back up at her ladyship, who had somehow managed to leverage herself one-handed higher up the fountain and was clinging to the spout. She kicked her left leg into the air, picked something up from the smallest fountain bowl, and held it aloft.

"Atcha!" she said, and looked down over her shoulder. "Ah, my drink."

With a slight push and a flutter of her silken skirts, her ladyship dropped back down to the ground. Her hair swirled and hit Ibram in the side; he crossed his arms over his chest. She landed without a sound, bending her knees for balance, and straightened up in time for the servant to reach them. He could see a filthy wire frame held between her thumb and forefinger of her left hand.

She rubbed the fingers of her right hand together as if to clean them and leaned over to smell the steam rising from the cup. "Caffa," she said, and blinked in surprise. "I didn't think the Northerners would have any. What a good choice, thank you." She smiled.

The servant bobbed her a bow. "Thank you, ladyship," she muttered. "Cook keeps a little tin just for the locals, you see."

"You're a Limmard, aren't you?" Lady Azadiya asked. "I've seen you in the marketplace. What are you doing serving drinks? I would have thought you'd be in the bakehouse."

The servant—Ibram looked closer. She had brown hair tucked in a simple bun braided with an orange ribbon, tan skin, and wore a plain gambeson and breeches. She did sort of look like Mistress Limmard, he supposed, but all their children were still doing sums in the Bedris school last he'd known.

"Yes, ladyship," she said. "I'm Trida."

Lady Azadiya nodded and picked up her cup of caffa by the handle. "When did you contract with the Halfrey? They crossed under the gate in the heart of the Feast of the Sundered Legion, I'm told, and—"

Trida shimmered with a sudden flare of red across her freckled cheeks. She gave a little jump and the paper-wrapped twists of honey drops skittered over her tray. "No, ladyship! I wouldn't try for work during the Feast, I swear! I came in just for the party, really. Marshal Steward Pherick sent word to the Master of Notices at the Scribes' Bureau, and they set the poster on the village board. They're paying extra on account of the short notice."

Lady Azadiya nodded and sipped her drink. Now that she mentioned it, Ibram could smell the rich, toasted fragrance of caffa. He breathed in a little more deeply; it'd been five years since he'd last had a taste.

"I didn't know we had caffa," he said.

Trida looked at him out of the corner of her eye. "Well, sir," she said. "Cook said he doesn't like to bring it out for the guardsmen. Says it makes you all shake like bowls of posset, and then you get into the stores for the honey drops, and—"

"Yes, thank you, I think I've got the idea," he interrupted.

"To be fair, it's why your ama never gave you any," Lady Azadiya said.

"I was a child!"

She shook her head. "So precocious. Now, Trida, do you know what this is?"

She held up the little wire frame in her other hand. It wavered in the air. Ibram leaned in more closely. The frame was small, with one longer oval headed by a smaller globe, all covered in blackened residue with red fluff popping up here and there. Little burnt pods swung from the frames, three in the larger oval and one in the middle of the globe.

"It's got red bits stuck to it," he said. "Paper?"

"It's probably fabric, sir. It's fraying," Trida said. "It's got... oh, what's this?"

She reached out, and ladyship pulled it out of her reach. Trida dropped her hands with a nervous tightening of her lips.

"It's the remains of the cursebird," Ibram said. He glanced back at the ruined fountain. "I thought they exploded into nothing once they were done."

"The *vessel*," Lady Azadiya reminded him. "And cursebirds do. Automatons do not. They fizzle, mostly, once the igniting resonance is expended with the fuel. Did you see where it came from, Trida?"

Trida swallowed and looked between them. "Well, no," she said. "Not really. I was laying out some laundry in the back of the courtyard and ran in when the screaming began."

"And it was in the servants' courtyard, bashing itself into things," Ibram said. He tucked his loose button back into his gambeson again, and watched another one unravel.

Trida looked between them again. "Well," she said, and swallowed. "When I came in, it was by the door and Olla was after it with a broom, and then the broom caught on fire, but the fire was blue of all things, and then the guards came rushing in, and—well, I'm sorry my lady, but I lost sight of it, really."

"So you never got near it?" Lady Azadiya asked. She sipped her caffa delicately.

Trida shook her head. "No, my lady."

"But Olla did," her ladyship murmured, and waggled the frame in her fingers. Grit flaked off into her green palm, and then fell to the ground. "She is unlucky, is Olla?"

Trida paused and then said, "I couldn't say, ladyship. She's been clumsy these past few days, but I suppose it's understandable."

Lady Azadiya nodded slowly. "Yes, it would be."

Ibram nodded. "Lots of that going around, unfortunately," he said. He reached out. "May I see that, my lady?"

Lady Azadiya stepped back and took the frame with her. "No," she said. "I'll keep hold of it awhile yet. Now." She tossed the last of her drink back with the tilt of her head and set the empty cup back on Trida's serving tray. "Thank you for helping me, Trida. You can go back to the servants' courtyard. I expect they're missing you."

Trida bowed and withdrew with one last look at Ibram from the corner of her eye. He waited until she was off the grass and back to the platform before gesturing at the filthy frame. "You can't think Trida had anything to do with it," he said.

Lady Azadiya seemed startled. "Don't be silly, of course I don't," she said. "If she had, something would have happened to her, and nothing has, has it? Her clothes were intact, not a hair out of place. And she carried that tray without incident."

"So...Olla, then?" he asked. "Because her broom caught fire?"

And she'd almost lost an entire stack of expensive glass bowls. He closed his mouth on that bit of information, though. He remembered her from the caravan journey; she was a Northerner and very excitable. She had enough trouble to deal with for the party; her ladyship sailing over to ask questions would just make her more nervous.

Instead of answering, her ladyship held the frame up to her eye level and stared at it. She chewed one corner of her mouth and pursed her lips. "I believe there's a maker's stamp on this," she said. "Look at the middle pouch, here."

She tilted the frame towards him, and Ibram swallowed. He bent closer and squinted, trying to see what she saw through the burnt sludge clinging to the little leather sack. It wavered in the breeze, and he caught a faint whiff of saltpeter.

He wrinkled his nose and stepped back. "I can't see anything, really," he said. "Maybe...a triangle?"

She hummed and nodded. "A four-sided regular solid, to be sure," she said. "This came out of that stall near Book Row. You know the one, in the alley behind the Imperial Mail."

"Oh you can't see that," he protested.

"Yes, I can!" she said and stuck it in his face. "Don't you remember buying a brace of these when you were younger? We primed them with luck trinkets, and stuck them in the eaves."

"Of course I remember, but you cannot!" he replied and took a further step away. He wiped his face with the flat of his palm reflexively. "You cannot tell where it's from based on half a burnt sigil. It's oozing with...whatever was inside of it, and it smells like the bottom of a pond."

"You know what this means, Ibram?" She grinned. "It's a stickum."

He blinked. "No, it isn't."

"It is."

"But it flew!"

She groaned. "This pedantic streak you've developed is unbecoming."

The opposite door to the public courtyard opened just then, and a stream of servants carrying trays of empty plates and bowls and cups came pouring through. Ibram turned to watch them and then looked back to Lady Azadiya. She held the little frame down by her side; a shiver of black dust now lay over the golden lace of her skirt. Through the open door, they could hear several shouts and a great splash. Ibram winced.

"Hang it, it's the ice wine," he said. His heartbeat throbbed in his ears for a moment. "Time to return to the public, I think."

Her ladyship laughed. "Did someone go fishing?"

They hurried to the open door, and Ibram gestured to the servants to make way. They scuttled back from the threshold as he walked over it. Over their heads, he could see a crowd had gathered around one of the little bridges over the interior pond in the center of the courtyard garden.

They ran closer, and Ibram's breath lurched in his chest. There sat the huge chilling frame of the ice wine held up by an enormous trestle table in the center of the main lawn, bracketed by Lally and a trio of guards, with that contortionist posing atop it. It looked fine, which...was something, he supposed. The Halfreys were a house of closefisted fools, but that would have been a loss the household could not survive.

Beyond them, however, someone—either several some-ones, or one very large one—was splashing and squawking in the water of the interior pond like a dipperbird after its supper. He groaned as Lady Azadiya passed him and headed directly for the commotion.

"Away, away, away," she chanted, waving her free hand in front of her, and the crowd of bemused partygoers parted obediently if not so obligingly. He trailed after her, one hand wrapped around his sica, until they reached the edge of the pond. A mechanical fish lay on its side on the grassy bank, the tiny bellows inside of it causing it to puff into an iridescent white ball and then deflate. He toed it back into the water and watched it wriggle off into the underwater grasses.

Ibram looked up and immediately bit both of his lips together. He breathed through the jump of laughter in his chest and threw it back down his throat. In the pond near the remains of the little decorative wooden bridge stood—or, well, tried to stand—a circle of three young lords from the outer villages, utterly drenched in water and brown with the sludge from the bottom of the pond. One of them—possibly a Vo Wolly from what remained dry of his pink-edged tunic—raised a dripping hand to his friend who had managed to stand. They both yanked at the same time, their shoulders straining visibly, but the Vo Wolly had the strength, and so toppled his would-be rescuer, who went splat over his friend's lap.

The crowd roared with laughter, and Ibram pressed his hand over his mouth. A buzzing group of pink and green-clad servants flitted on the edges of the pond, clearly neither willing to help their employers out nor to leave them to their fate. The third man, wet from the crown of his rather old-fashioned braid to the bottoms of his boots, put both hands on his hips and rubbed his face; mud smeared him, and Ibram could hear the noise of disgust even over the crowd. The littlest Vo Wolly stood as tall as she was able and bowed to the party to laughing applause before she began making her way to the bank of the pond. The partygoers jostled back and forth as they all watched the rest of them slog their way to shore. The largest stood there, dripping, with his arms outstretched until several maids launched towels in his direction.

"Oh no," Lord Sans said, high and a bit breathless, and Ibram saw him appear at the end of the broken bridge with Ahksell in tow. His face was red and his whole head seemed to shake with outrage. "Oh this is—Pherick! Marshal Steward Pherick! What is going on—who broke this bridge?" he began to shout, and Ibram saw Ahksell bending down to speak softly to him. The young lord closed his mouth, but he shivered and began twisting the fingers of his left hand with his right. Ibram thought he saw the Marshal Steward inching his way towards the door with his head down.

The mood of the crowd began to lose its merriment and a horde of servants descended with towels, distinctly not followed by a blank-faced Marshal Steward Pherick. The servants led the afflicted up from the bank and onto the more solid grass; restorative drinks were applied, and one of the Vo Wolly laughed aloud. Ibram caught Lady Azadiya's eye and nodded at Lord Sans. She pursed her lips. As people began to draw away from the pond, she walked toward Lord Sans' group, still carrying the little bedraggled stickum frame.

Lord Sans quivered in rage on the walkway, almost glaring after the now-swaddled Vo Wollys. Ahksell bowed with a small, relieved sigh. "Mentor," he said as he straightened. "I think this..." he glanced around and lowered his voice. "This curse might be gaining strength!"

Ibram watched a small tic develop in Lord Sans' left eye and sighed.

"It's ruined," Lord Sans muttered. "It's all ruined, and I'll..." He trailed off and became pale.

"The damp again, ladyship?" Ibram asked, and felt a small, tingling welling of an emotion that was possibly a second cousin of pity for the young lord. He looked like a spool of yarn a cat had got its claws into. A glance at Ahksell saw him frowning at the water; he had always had a soft and forgiving heart.

Lady Azadiya did not answer; she was watching Lord Sans. Ibram coughed. She made a humming noise. "Oh, yes, actually. It's an old manor."

Ibram felt his eyebrows shoot up his forehead.

"*Damp?*" Lord Sans repeated. He pointed. "The bridge is gone!"

"Only that side of it, and they were clearly playing too close to the edge. I know those boys. They were terrors at school. Ahksell, where have you been?" she asked.

Ahksell had a furrow in his forehead, but it cleared when

he spoke. "Lord Sans took me to his cellar," he said. "It's a marvelous trick that the Sect Above the Clouds has created. It's not as cold as it was, so I'm told, but it's still covered in frost. I tried—with permission from lordship, I mean—I had a small cup of the ice wine itself."

"Did you?" she asked. "Here, Lord Sans, hold this."

She held out the little frame, and the man took it automatically. He stared down at the filthy thing and blinked in confusion. Lady Azadiya watched him carefully. Ibram sighed and glanced around the rest of the public courtyard. The sounds of a great number of people being offered free alcohol and small amounts of food were growing. He imagined the Marshal Steward was caught in the throng, or possibly drowning himself inside it.

"It's delicious," Ahksell was saying when Ibram returned his attention to the group. "I felt an immediate tingle in my hands and face, and even the reports of renewed energy seem to be true! I can see why San—Lord Sans is so proud of it!"

"Indeed so," she said. "Lord Sans?"

"Yes, ladyship?" Lord Sans murmured. He had turned slightly dewy-eyed as Ahksell did the job of selling his most expensive offering to his own Mentor. A thin, high flush rode his cheekbones.

Ibram cleared his throat, and Lord Sans snapped out of his admiring haze.

"Are you proud of your ice wine?" she asked.

"I am, ladyship," Lord Sans said with a quick nod and a bob of his throat. "I'm the first of my family to travel this far from Halfrilat, and it's *very* important to my father."

"A tasking gentleman, I've heard," she said.

Lord Sans swallowed heavily, and she nodded slowly. "I found your problem," she said.

Lord Sans looked surprised. "You did?"

"Of course," she said. "Have you seen one of those before?"

He lifted the battered frame, and she nodded. He shook his head. "It looks like a...one of those things you get on Derlive's Night. They buzz around and breathe colored sparks."

"We call them stickums here," Ahksell said. He leaned over Lord Sans' shoulder. "But we can get them any old time, really. You buy them empty and then fill in the proper ingredients for...well, for birthdays or weddings or store openings, that sort of thing. They're for luck and can carry a limited resonance cantrip. They have expendable resin in their little pots and you light the tail with—"

"I thank you, Ahksell," her ladyship interrupted.

"Mentor," Ahksell muttered, and settled back on his heels.

"And this is the problem?" Lord Sans asked. He twiddled the little frame in his fingers. "It's...not a curse?"

"What do they teach you in the North?" Lady Azadiya said flatly. "No, as I keep saying. It's a cantrip, and a fairly benign one at that. It said...what did it say, Ibram?"

"Go home, or make diamonds from snow," he said. "Stay and...stay and rot?"

"He's possessed of such a wonderful memory," she said. "It's a quality hard to come by."

"*That* is benign?" Lord Sans asked. His wide set eyes showed a bit too much white for polite company. "Do you know what it took to get my caravan down here? We can't just pack up our wagons and run back to Halfrilat with only a few low river contracts under our belts!"

Ibram ground his teeth. Those 'low river contracts' had been the result of Lord Sans' inability to pass a manor house without stopping for an introduction. By tradition a noble could claim refuge with others of similar rank on their travels. They'd slowly wound their way from the Bright Broken Peaks up to the Salt Plateau and down again to the farming valleys at the foot of the Emerald Mountains while the young lord stretched his legs on the imperial roads, free of parents, older siblings, and good sense. He'd made a reputation, if not an acceptable amount of coin.

"It's open-ended," she answered. "You arrived in all apparent good health. I have seen no further evidence of rot than a poor cheese—"

"What happened to the cheese?" Lord Sans asked.

Lady Azadiya ignored him. "The script is not at all specific, and the very weakness of the cantrip says it wasn't meant to cause any real harm."

"But the bridge!" Lord Sans exclaimed.

"Oh, it's nothing but two feet from the ground—"

"Water," Ibram muttered.

Her thumb and forefinger pinched, and Ibram winced at the invisible tug on his ear. He slapped his palm over the sore spot and rubbed.

"And those Vo Wollys are more muscle than bone," her ladyship said, "perfectly safe to land in a bit of sludge."

"And clothes wash," Ahksell pointed out.

Lady Azadiya nodded approvingly. "Just so."

Lord Sans sighed loudly. "I suppose we'll have to pay for the laundry, as well."

A short silence developed, because what could anyone say to that? Ibram barely withstood the urge to roll his eyes and instead fixed them over the greater party beyond. The excitement of the pond over, most of them had returned to talking and drinking, exactly as Lord Sans had no doubt hoped. The smaller bridges covering the rest of the interior pond, however, were definitely free of people. Ibram frowned.

"This is quite a party," Mistress Tarsis said behind Ibram's shoulder. "Ample selection of drinks, perfectly acceptable food, and even a bit of a show."

Lady Azadiya turned with a welcoming expression, and Ibram stepped out of the way so that the Tarsises could make their bows to her ladyship. His heels sank into the ground in the uneven grass. Lord Sans drew up and puffed out his chest; his face blotched with color. Mistress Tarsis held two cups, mostly full, in either hand, and her husband held none. Somewhere along the way they'd lost their trailing group of admirers.

"I see you've been helping yourself," Lord Sans said with his nose in the air.

"I didn't think you had enough staff for everyone to be served individually," Mistress Tarsis replied.

Lord Sans opened his mouth, but Lady Azadiya cut in like the Mistress of a middling House who sees her son about to step outside with the tailor's apprentice. "How have you both been?" she asked. "I must admit I didn't expect to see you here of all places."

Mistress Tarsis nodded; her curls bounced. "We are both quite well, thank you, Mentor Hobon," she said, putting a slight stress on Lady Azadiya's secondary title. "Our invitation quite caught us off guard, but it's always nice to welcome new folk to the village."

"How neighborly," Lord Sans said, in a voice almost as sour as the smell in the air.

A few servants arrived with large fans in their hands and began to move the air about them. The sailing lights took flight across the garden. Ibram felt his lips begin to curl upward, and forced them back down again. He squared his shoulders instead, while trying to get his right heel out of the muck without anyone taking notice.

"Were you aware of Lord San's arrival?" Lady Azadiya asked. "It's been a twelve day or more since I've seen your carriage climb up the living mountain." She clasped her hands over her stomach, sending her sleeves to billow out at her sides. Ibram lifted one heel out of the grass to redistribute his weight and heard a slight sucking sound. His other foot sank precariously.

"Our house's representative at the Delbrite port asked my lord Juba to make a personal inspection of the shipments coming up from Vissiliat," Mistress Tarsis said. "Two shiploads of Kinnanbrite red! I decided to come along as well."

"All the way from Delbrite?" Lady Azadiya asked. "You must have made good time on the roads. That's at least a seven day journey from here."

The Tarsises shared a glance, amused but cautious. Master Tarsis raised both hands and signed. From the corner of his eye, Ibram saw Lord Sans fiddling with the little stickum frame, and then wiping the fingers of his left hand on his breeches.

"It was, ladyship," Mistress Tarsis said, with one eye on her husband. "We left not...quite after the Feast of the Sundered Legion."

"Well, a subject of the Empire can ignore such petty festivals," Lady Azadiya said, and Ibram saw hope glow in Lord Sans' eyes.

"Really?" he asked. "Ucalegon told me they were incredibly important."

"Of course, we would never leave without it being on very important business," Mistress Tarsis' voice bobbled, but she rallied. "The manager is a thorough man. We were forced to spend a day and a night at our home in Delbrite. I'm afraid we only arrived in Lityen yesterday. Another day and we would have missed the fortune of Lord Sans' invitation to the party!"

Master Tarsis signed something quickly, smiling, and Lady Azadiya laughed. "Yes, that's true," she said.

She nodded at Lord Sans, who was beginning to look a

little pale, and said, "Master Tarsis is aiding one of the Attendants in the Preceptory of Bedris in a study, you see. He's building—attempting to create—a kind of voice box which will use the Imperial Language of Sign. So that Master Tarsis won't have to rely on others to translate for him all the time."

"Not that I mind helping when necessary," Mistress Tarsis interjected. Her husband lifted the glass from her left hand and toasted her, and she smiled at him as he took a drink. He handed it back to her just as a draft of green smoke wafted over from the water clock. Ibram's nose twitched at the herbal stench.

"He was noting how handy it would be right now," Lady Azadiya said.

"What, the—Master Tarsis signs something, and then someone else reads it aloud?" Lord Sans asked.

Mistress Tarsis laughed. "Yes, I suppose, lordship, but then the voice reading it stays...oh, well, I presume forever, but I have no knowledge of such things," she said. "I believe Attendant Zafer is using his own voice currently. So that he can make corrections as needed later on."

"Your house has a...very close relationship to the sect, then?" Lord Sans asked. He sucked a corner of his mouth briefly.

"For years and years and years," Mistress Tarsis said.

"So long as that?" Lady Azadiya replied. "I do hope you aren't bored with your contract."

Master Tarsis signed something very quickly and emphatically, holding both hands at his chest.

"We could never be bored with an arrangement that is so pleasant to both parties. It is our honor to serve the Sect of Seven Fires," Mistress Tarsis translated. "Our cellars are ever at your disposal."

"And I'm sure Mistress Mahnaz continues to be pleased," Lady Azadiya said.

Master Tarsis nodded with a smile.

"Mistress Mahnaz?" Lord Sans asked.

Ibram winced. Marshal Steward Pherick closed his eyes briefly. Mistress Tarsis' eyebrows twitched, but Master Tarsis placed a hand on her side.

"Mistress Mahnaz is the Minister of Procurement for the Sect of Seven Fires, lord," Ahksell said. "She's really very nice."

And she had been sent an invitation, which had been politely refused; Ibram had seen the note. Mistress Mahnaz had a great deal to do before the Festival of the Founder, and little enough time to do it with it coming so soon after the Feast of the Sundered Legion. Most of the wine and spirits were ordered beforehand simply to save time, which was why this exhibition was filled by young lords and ladies, and small house contractmen hungry for an exotic edge.

"I'll have to meet her someday, then," Lord Sans said.

"You may send a letter," Lady Azadiya said. "We have an entire scribes' bureau up the living mountain, and our own postmaster."

"Up the...living mountain?" Lord Sans repeated.

"It's how folk refer to the Sect of Seven Fires, lordship," Ibram reminded him. It was a habit by now. "Because it's covered in trees and alchemists."

Ahksell laughed. "Like an ant hill!"

Lady Azadiya shook her head but smiled. Master Tarsis signed to his wife, who handed over his wine. He sipped deeply from his wine glass and then pinched his lips together. Ibram held his breath. Master Tarsis swallowed, licked his lips, and then shuddered. Lord Sans swayed and turned red as he watched Master Tarsis hand his wife his now empty glass and give a short bow. His two broad hands flexed as he signed at chest height.

"If you will excuse us," Mistress Tarsis said quickly.

"Of course," Lady Azadiya said, just as Lord Sans popped open his mouth.

"Your brew is an acquired taste, lordship," Mistress Tarsis said, as they began to walk down the wooden platform to return to the crowd. Mistress Tarsis firmly shoved her glasses into the hands of a passing maid. They disappeared into the throng, but not before Ibram saw Master Tarsis put his hand to his stomach, and shudder.

"Oh no," muttered Lord Sans. He signaled to a passing waiter with an empty tray. "Oh no."

"That went well," Ibram said quietly, and then glanced at Lord Sans from the corner of his eye.

"Quite the Ruckus," Lady Azadiya said with her eyes on the crowd, who were slowly swirling around the water clock again.

"Mentor," Ahksell said.

She turned to him. "Yes?"

"I think—I mean, I wonder if—Watch out!"

The ground gave way underneath Ibram's weight; it felt like he was stepping backwards into pudding. Ahksell grabbed him by one arm and hauled him straight. They rebounded off each other, but Ibram managed to get one foot on the platform and the other on more solid ground. He wavered but disentangled himself from Ahksell and leaned his elbow on his raised knee. The others stared at him. He tucked his hand under his chin nonchalantly.

Ahksell clapped his hands together. "Well, there's a thing. You must have gotten very close to that stickum."

"What? I suppose so," Ibram said.

Lord Sans nodded. He still looked flushed and kept tugging at his gambeson. "He was...you were there in the courtyard, weren't you, Ucalegon? When the cursebird, I should say, the *stickum*, flew in."

"Yes, lordship," Ibram said.

"Honestly," Lady Azadiya said loudly. "Who were these gardeners? Come, move along, before Ahksell winds up with a mechanical fish down his breeches again."

"*Mentor.*"

"You are cursed with my memory of your every deed and it's high time you became used to it. Ibram, take your leg down, you look like a riverman."

Ibram set his leg down with a thump. Well now, that was unfair, really. He'd caught his balance as best he could, and it was—the ground had fallen away from him, after all. He grumbled to himself and crossed his arms over his chest. She continued speaking without taking much notice of his discontent.

"Lord Sans, do you think you could find your Marshal Steward for me? I have a need to speak to him. We shall be in the next smaller garden terrace." Lord Sans puffed his chest up and opened his mouth. She held out her hand. "I shall need that frame again."

Lord Sans deflated and shut his mouth. He held up the frame, and she took it from him. Lady Azadiya nodded briskly and began to walk away across the grass with the frame twisting between her fingers. Ibram and Ahksell hurriedly made their bows and stumbled after her. Her skirts rustled as she walked, flowing back and almost tangling their legs. Ibram swerved left and jumped up to a clear space on the walkway as Lady Azadiya ascended the stairs with Ahksell at her heels.

The crowd was louder now that the wine and ale had been passed around. The circlers had struck up another dancing round, and a crowd of young lords—some still damp—had joined hands to dance. The jugglers were being tossed hunks of bread from a tray held by a pair of Ealers. The air felt close; it smelled of spilled wine and something sweet, like cake. It made a nice change from the previous miasma, but the shift was disconcerting. Ibram swallowed as he followed Lady Azadiya down the long wooden walkway.

She walked swiftly as they made their way through the party, and Ibram found his breath quickening in his chest. What had she found out? He looked about him, but saw no destruction or oddly colored steam as they walked further down the public courtyard.

The outer terraces were still within the walls, but separated into private bowers and small gardens. The sailing lights cast warm, golden shadows on the less populated walkways. This portion was well-tended, and the bushes were allowed to grow head-high to give a pretense of seclusion. There were pyrus trees and flowering shrubs and low benches.

Lady Azadiya paused in the center of a roundel of benches circling a small, burbling fountain dedicated to the Runner. Ahksell stopped at her elbow and Ibram slowed to a halt a few feet at her left. She looked up at the statue's well-carved feet and then down at the stickum frame in her right hand. With her left, she twisted the two wires that formed the globe while she breathed on the frame. It glowed green for a moment.

"It really was a smart thought," she said. "To allow yourself to be so afflicted."

"Mentor?" Ahksell asked.

Ibram straightened his back where he'd begun to slouch.

She turned and threw the frame in the air. It hovered, twisting right and then left, and burned a cherry red. Ibram smelled smoke; he caught it as it flew into his chest. It chirped, a single note like a high bell, and shivered in his hands like a live thing. He yelled and tossed it to the ground, scraping his palms against each other. The little stickum frame crumbled to ash and then to nothing.

"Are you all right, Ibram?" Ahksell asked. He hurried over and took both of Ibram's palms in his, turning them over, knuckles to palms. He sighed. "You don't look hurt. Mentor, really, you must watch where you throw. Why did you do that?"

Ibram chuckled a little too breathlessly for his own comfort. "One of the little bags must have had something left in it," he said.

"I think I'm a little disappointed in you. *That*," she said, "is how you dispose of evidence. You know very well that stickums always leave something behind unless you clean up after yourself."

Ahksell and he both paused and looked at each other and then at her. Ibram closed his suddenly dry mouth and tugged his hands from Ahksell's grip. He placed them behind his back.

"I beg your pardon?" he asked.

She raised one eyebrow. "Honestly, Ibram," she said. "A *stickum*?"

He took a step back. "What?"

She walked closer, brushing her green-dyed hands free of detritus. "When they're the silliest things in the world, barely a babe's toy. Although, truly"—she paused and tugged on one long strand of her hair—"I do suppose you've reminded me of a valuable lesson."

He swallowed and took another step back, only to be stopped by Ahksell's grip on his elbow. "And what's that?"

"You can weaponize anything. Am I proud? Am I furious?" she asked. Mostly, she just seemed overwhelmingly amused, which made all the muscles in Ibram's back turn to stone and then water. He would have winced, but she marched onwards. "I think I will decide later. Ahksell, take note. I'm sure this will come back up later in your life, as it has in mine."

"Yes, Mentor," Ahksell said. He sounded grim.

"Oh, hang it," Ibram mutter and shook himself free. "I've

been nothing but helpful to these people since their post-master stole my letters and their manor guard chained me up in their storeroom. They rifled through all my personal belongings! Six years was removed from my lifespan after six minutes in that place."

"Ibram, you didn't," Ahksell said.

Ibram stuck his chin in the air. "And wouldn't I have had cause? But instead, I've been running around Lityen, making sure this party gets all its due."

Lady Azadiya nodded. "Oh, indeed," she said. "And it's well you have. Otherwise what greater audience would you be playing this prank to? Just the young lord alone, and whatever servants got caught up in it. Really, Ib-la, poor Olla."

A fizzing sensation erupted from his stomach and buzzed through the rest of his body. He shook his head and scrubbed the back of his neck with his right hand. "I'm sorry about the servants getting caught up in this, but that was not my fault."

She waggled her head. "And yet."

He raised both hands up to his chest. "It wasn't! I can't be blamed for who gets near a stickum when they're flying around; I got a good whack at it myself!"

He tugged on his gambeson and three knots unraveled at once like they'd practiced it. Ahksell rolled his eyes, and Ibram resisted the urge to make a face in his general direc-tion. He began piecing his clothing back together.

"Your gambeson," Ahksell said.

Ibram looked up to see her ladyship nod encouragingly.

"You forgot your half-cloak," Ahksell said. "Then that tray of glasses, and when did you get that stain on your breeches?"

"That was the fault of you and your addiction to sweets," Ibram said. "How many milk buns have you had today?"

"I have a perfectly normal relationship to desserts, thank you," Ahksell said. "And don't change the subject!"

"Everyone who got close to the stickum as it flew has

been plagued with clumsiness," she interrupted. "Then, my poor not-so-little Ibram has suddenly forgotten the care of his clothing? What better way to hide whatever ill luck rubbed off on you setting the stickum off, than getting close to it while it flew about in a pretense of helpfulness?"

Lady Azadiya stood there, tall and shining, and tossed her hair over one shoulder. Ibram felt the kick of his heartbeat begin to pound against his ribcage. Ahksell crossed his unfortunately broad arms over his chest.

"What did you call it again?" Lady Azadiya asked. "In your invitation?"

"The Ruckus," Ibram said.

"It is just a ruckus, isn't it?" She nodded and came closer, ticking items off on her green fingers with every step. "Nothing of note, and nothing to harm. A bit of irritation...a hit to the pocketbook, maybe a good dose of humiliation for the young lord from Halfrilat." She twisted her lips together into a smile. "A few days of panic for—how long were you in their storeroom?"

His gut soured a bit at the reminder. It had been cold and dusty, and there had been no light in that storeroom, just the skittering sound of rock mice. "Three days."

"Not a very high rate of return, my dear," she said. "For all the turmoil that must have caused you." She swayed closer to him, and the hem of her garments brushed his legs. "I confess, had I not received your invitation, I would have been far more angry than intrigued."

"It's still not right," Ahksell said. "What if someone had gotten hurt? Those Vo Wollys could have landed wrong, you know."

"Yes," she nodded slowly. "I've noticed some curdled faces amongst the throng, but surely not enough to flatten Lord Sans' purse, really. Most of them were perfectly happy."

Ibram rubbed his thumbnail along his right eyebrow. He

glanced from Ahksell to Lady Azadiya. He swallowed. "Well. I'm older now, you see. I've learned how to frame things."

"If that was a pun, I'm leaving," Ahksell said.

"This, sadly, does represent a maturation of your character," her ladyship agreed.

"What did you say?" Ahksell asked. "Or put in? A stickum has to have a script."

Ibram shrugged. "I didn't say anything!"

Her dark eyes held Ibram's steadily. His jaw worked. He nodded and clasped and unclasped his hands.

"What was the cantrip you used?" she asked.

"I don't know what cantrip was used to set it off, only what it said."

"Almost diplomatic," Lady Azadiya said, and narrowed her eyes slightly. "Since you write scripts for cantrips rather than speak them aloud. Like your invitation, which you absolutely switched out from whatever mush they would have used. No Marshal Steward would have allowed 'come have a glass and figure out a pernicious curse.' When I am nothing to do with curses or blessings at all? *Ibram*."

A grin curled the corners of his mouth, and he was helpless to prevent it. "My employers requested your invitation. As an understanding."

She snorted and rolled her eyes. "So you risk a fined dismissal to get me here?"

"Well, you said yourself you hate parties."

She paused, and then her eyes widened. "Ibram," she said. "Was this all for my amusement?"

"No," he protested. "Not...all of it."

She pinched the bridge of her nose and sighed.

Ibram spread his hands in a helpless gesture. "Seven months, I wasted in that caravan," he said. "Listening to the young lord wax on about Western barbarians and wane pale with disinterest when I tried to tell him otherwise. He could have floated down the Sig with the amount of his own wine he drank, and never once did he think I didn't want to be there, just because they didn't lock me up for a spy."

Lady Azadiya dropped her hand from her face and brushed her palms together. "And you are not a dog," she said. "To be pacified with treats, even in such a relatively pleasant house as this."

He shook his head.

"And yet a deal is a deal, to be sure," Lady Azadiya said. "So Lord Sans Halfrey's invitation is brought to me. I have decided to give you the compliment of understanding quite rightly that I'd ignore anyone else attached to this house."

"And then," Ahksell said slowly, "on one of those trips that so intrigued the village, you picked the stickum up in the old shop. Then you... I've got it!

"You used Alfrin powder instead of gold dust, Illith salts for the color, and something base instead of noble, something...zinc? For the duration? The ignition would have come with the frame, but you'd have had to write out the cantrip *and* the script itself...which is how they understood it! You know all their sayings! You've been north!" Ahksell stopped with a grin.

Ibram glanced at her ladyship, who tilted her head. Ahksell bounced on his toes. Ibram waggled his head back and forth.

Ahksell groaned. "Oh now, you must say it," he said. "You must tell me where you put the thing!"

"Where has Ucalegon put what?" Lord Sans asked, and Ibram's stomach dropped into his shoes.

Lady Azadiya's eyes widened. She whirled to face the entrance to the little secluded benches, where Marshal Steward Pherick and Lord Sans and the Imperial Commissioner stood. Ibram nearly groaned aloud. Yilka the Green had three faces and luck was most assuredly turned away from him. A precious, lurching heartbeat of silence passed, and then Lady Azadiya's arms spread wide.

"Lady Sebbina!" she said brightly. "How delightful. Are you enjoying the party?"

Lady Sebbina stumped into the clearing, and Ibram took several judicious steps backwards. Ahksell stood by his side. Their eyes met and then darted away.

"But what were you saying to Attendant Solari?" Lord Sans asked. He seemed a little flushed. "Where did he put what?"

Ibram tensed. He'd been away five years, after all, and Ahksell was soft-hearted. His stomach turned over, just a lurching twitch of muscle. He looked over at him and swallowed.

"A present!" Ahksell said, wide-eyed. He tucked his arms behind his back. "I'm an old friend of the family, you know."

Ibram sucked in too much air and coughed it out again. "It's true," he said. "I brought him..." A vast and empty slate welled up in his mind's eye, light as an empty purse. What did Ahksell even like these days? Tree-climbing? Not cheese. A wheel fiddle? "Well, it will spoil the surprise now, but..."

"Oh no," Ahksell said, a tad too late. He shook his head briskly. "I love surprises! I don't need—don't tell me. It's just...nice having you home."

Ahksell's shoulders slumped for a second, and Ibram's mouth parted just a little. Ahksell shrugged minutely. "Just a full story would be enough for me," Ahksell said.

Ibram paused. "Yes," he said, finally, and cleared his throat. "Yes, I can do that. I've got so much to tell you! There's...there was this mutt on the Salt Plateau that—"

A cleared throat brought Ibram back to recognition of his company. He turned to Marshal Steward Pherick, who seemed to have regained his calm, but was now watching them with narrowed eyes. What exactly had they heard? Lord

Sans opened his mouth, but Lady Sebbina's walking stick thumped on the ground.

Ahksell elbowed him, and they bowed to Lady Sebbina with their arms at their stomachs. Having the cane, she only used one arm, but it was enough to raise them back up. Ibram bowed additionally to Lord Sans and Marshal Steward Pherick, who waved him off.

"My Attendant very much missed Ibram on his travels," Lady Azadiya said. "Please excuse their youthful enthusiasm."

"The young belong at such parties," Lady Sebbina said. "And I grow tired. I saw you making the rounds, Lady Azadiya."

She smiled. "I enjoy a lively spirit, ladyship," she said.

Lady Sebbina resettled her grip on her walking stick and snorted. "As I have been told." She turned her sharp eyes to Ibram. "Are you still carrying her water, boy?"

A short, strangled laugh erupted from Ahksell. Ibram elbowed him, hard. "I'm an arm-for-hire, ladyship," he said. "I go where the money is."

She nodded. "And your whole family before you," she observed.

"Not entirely so," Lady Azadiya pointed out with a smile that dipped tightly.

Lady Sebbina scoffed, but said no more about it. "Have you concluded your business here? I would speak with you, Azadiya, as several of my previous messages have seemed to have gone astray."

Lady Azadiya hid her hands in the folds of her dress, but her smile regained its brilliance. "But of course, my lady," she said. "I am always at your disposal."

"Oh, but you'll miss the presentation of the ice wine!" Lord Sans protested. "Lady Sebbina, surely business can wait."

"I am not fond of sweet wines, Lord Sans." Lady Sebbina

said. She resituated her grip on her cane. "But we shall be back in due time. I thank you for leading me here, and for your hospitality. However, I need to speak with the Fourth Mentor in private, and I'm sure your guests have noticed your absence. Would you and the Marshal Steward be so kind as to take Azadiya's companions back with you?"

"Oh...of course, my lady," Lord Sans said. He swallowed. "I would be honored."

Lady Sebbina clearly could not have cared less, but she waved him away and walked with purpose over to the bench on the far side of the fountain. She sat down and wrapped both hands around the top of her stick. Lady Azadiya turned to follow and then twisted back on her heels.

"Ah, Marshal Steward," she said. "About our earlier conversation?"

Marshal Steward Pherick's face rippled with some soon repressed emotion, but he leaned forward quickly. "Yes, ladyship?"

"As I said, these troubles should go away on their own, but if it's truly a bother, I would suggest burning a ball of dragon's blood wrapped in muskroot wherever the item might have passed by. It should help clear the air."

"Do you mean that's all we had to do?" Lord Sans asked. He pulled on the back of his blond hair. "My second-best tunic was ruined! We had to commission two entirely new sets of dishware! And all we had to do was...was burn a little dragon's blood? Pherick, why didn't we attempt that? I cannot—"

Marshal Steward Pherick cleared his throat politely, and Lord Sans shut his mouth. "Does ladyship know where in Lityen such items can be acquired?"

"Ahksell can show you, lordship," Ibram said, as he watched the young lord turn puce. He *was* young, wasn't he? And soon gone from Ibram's sphere, any road. "The sect usually provides the ingredients through their quartermaster, and he knows how to make the thing correctly."

"I do," Ahksell said, a little too eagerly. "I can even find out the best place to set up your cleansing. There's so many places that could be useful, you know, we could—well, I beg your pardon, lordship, you would have to show me the afflicted areas."

"The eaves," Ibram offered, and Marshal Steward Pherick's eyes flickered towards him. His mouth tightened. "Since it went through the doorway between the more private courtyards."

Lord Sans nodded rapidly. "Oh yes!" he exclaimed. "I can show you now. We'll...show you, now, I mean to say."

He looked from Marshal Steward Pherick to Ibram and seemed to vibrate a little, caught between rushing off and staying in place politely. Ibram decided not to think on it. His contract would be over with this party, and with it the freedom he'd bargained from Ama before taking up his duties at the Sect of Seven Fires. On the morning, he would be repairing his clothes in his childhood home, probably while burning his own little ball of dragon's blood and muskroot near a very large and open window. He wrinkled his nose in remembrance of the smell.

"Well, that settles it," Lady Azadiya said. "Best to simply move on, I've always found. And, of course, Ahksell will deal with—work with you on my order. I shall have a case of that trembleberry, lordship, and a bottle of your ice wine as well."

Lord Sans' mouth opened and then closed. "You will?" he asked.

"Lady Azadiya," Lady Sebbina said in as close to a shout as Ibram had ever heard.

"Coming!" Lady Azadiya did not yell in return. She caught Ibram's eye, and he looked away. "Yes, Lord Sans. For your trouble in travel, and in light of fact that you have returned my agent to me, for which I thank you. Now, then, Ahksell, bargain well. Ibram, I shall see you in seven days' time."

"You will?" Ibram asked, startled.

"Of course," she said, dusting imaginary dirt from her green hands. "Your ama wishes you home for the Founder, your sister mentioned something about a present, and then I am to meet with your father on a new commission. It should give you plenty of time to reconnect. Really, what a lovely little party. So much to do! I've decided I'm quite pleased."

She walked over to Lady Sebbina and sat a little further down on the bench. He could hear her laugh. Marshal Steward Pherick eyed them all again but said nothing. Lord Sans attached himself to Ahksell's side immediately, already prattling about Lady Azadiya's order as they walked off. By the time they reached the main end of the courtyard, the entire party would know of the Fourth Mentor's private commission. A soured glass or six couldn't compete with that in the long run.

A warmth grew in the center of Ibram's chest, and he found himself hiding a grin by gazing down at his feet. He was home again. Tomorrow, he would be celebrating with his family. Perhaps he'd toss a few dice for Yilka the Green after all.

Across the grass, Lady Sebbina thumped her cane twice into the ground. He looked up, startled, and Lady Azadiya visibly sighed. Marshal Steward Pherick cleared his throat. Ibram jumped and turned around.

"You will perhaps accompany Attendant Solari and Lord Sans, Ucalegon," Pherick said. "While I attend to the party."

Ibram's eyes widened. "Me, Marshal Steward?"

"Indeed. I think we both know Lord Sans is prone to..." The Marshal Steward chewed on his next words. "Enthusiasm," he finally settled upon with a sigh.

Ibram's mouth twitched; he grinned. Ah yes. His part, it

seemed, wasn't completely over yet. He bowed to the Marshal Steward, and then followed the other man out of the garden area, and back into the throng.

⁂

Thank you for reading! And, if you've left a review for my work, thank you again! Reviews help others find my book.

Want a sneak peek of the next adventure in The Alchemist's Agent series? Turn the page for a look at the beginning of *The Gilty Party*!

THE GILTY PARTY: SNEAK PEEK

I bram Ucalegon rubbed the back of his neck as the swaying aerial gondola he traveled in rolled down its thick wire hauling rope. Their carriage shuddered to a halt on the track line at the relay station. A platform conductor held her hand up to the window while the gondola was redirected to the next line, and Ibram nodded, though he doubted she could see him. Beside him, Ahksell Solari, childhood friend and all-around fussbudget, leaned closer to the window and waved to the burly servants pushing their gondola from one section of the station to the next. He had to hunch down to do so, but Ahksell was both huge and friendly, and so never seemed to mind contorting into the oddest positions in order to fit in a courtesy.

"If you'd wanted breakfast, *Attendant* Solari," Ibram continued as he shuffled to the window screen next to the door to give Ahksell a little more breathing room. "You could have just eaten in your dormitory with the rest of your compatriots."

Ahksell grinned and shrugged. "But no one sets out a breakfast like your mother!"

Ibram rolled his eyes. They were alone in the carriage, which suited him well since that meant they could speak normally rather than whisper in order to spare the ears of their fellow passengers. Like many folk in the surrounding villages, Ibram's daily journey up the living mountain to the Sect of Seven Fires involved a carriage, two perpetual wheels, and a diversion from the imperial road through the deeply disturbing lift system which acted as the mountain's central transportation. It was rare that he had any space to breathe at all.

The aerial gondola rocked into its tracks as two different burly servants attached the spring-loaded grip to the hauling rope which rose up the mountain. Ibram swallowed heavily. Not that the air was doing him any good, regardless of personal space.

Ahksell waved at them as well, and then grabbed Ibram's shoulder for balance as they began to sway upwards. Ibram braced his feet; they both wobbled but soon found their footing again. The relay station dropped away from view.

"Besides," Ahksell protested, and Ibram tore his attention from the window. "Mentor Hobon wanted to speak with you, and I had no other plans."

"Which I would have learned when I went up the mountain without you needing to fetch me," Ibram pointed out. "Since I do that every morning. For my work."

Ahksell shrugged; it looked rather like a mountain range resettling itself. At all reports, while Ibram had been away, Ahksell's growth spurt had begun at and Ibram saw no evidence that it had stopped since. Ibram sniffed and turned back to the wire screen window. Deep green treetops waved beneath him; he grit his teeth. What a horrible way to travel.

Surely cutting a swath of roads up from the base of the mountain range had to be better than this—this lugging back and forth, like they were in the lunch pail of a giant walker.

Simply because Ibram had never seen a better system in all his travels didn't make the relays the best. Other kingdoms doubtless had their own methods. He glanced about himself while Ahksell began to hum a tune Ibram didn't recognize. Their carriage featured four large square wire screened windows—an amazing expense if they hadn't been made by the alchemists themselves. It provided Ibram an excellent view of the world and his little place within it.

If he could manage to maneuver himself around Ahksell to face the back he might see the village of Lityen, where he'd been born and raised. To his left—upwards of course—perched the Preceptory of Yseult, seventh domicile of the Sect of Seven Fires, pride of the Vissilian Empire, nestled within the Emerald Mountains on the most western edge of the province of Vanima, a haven for alchemists and academics, and the sort of folk who enjoyed setting fires to find out what might burn. Ibram, for his sins, was employed there in a more-or-less unofficial family tradition.

"You come down the living mountain and eat my ama's cooking, but you won't tell me what Ladyship wants, even though you expressly came to the house to tell me she wants me to come to work," Ibram said. "This was your plan."

Ahksell grinned. "You know the mentor," he said. "I didn't want to prejudice you about the Monbriths."

Mentor Hobon—or Lady Azadiya Hobon, as Ibram knew her—operated out of her tower in Yseult as its Fourth Mentor. The preceptory believed in the refinement of the physical body, which seemed to mean they drank a plethora of oddly colored, often smoking, infusions and then gained the ability to jump very high and float boulders out of farmer's fields. If they were very good at it, they might gain enough control to not require their potions and pills; Ibram didn't want to know how they achieved that. Ahksell might have told him, but Ibram had firmly decided never to inquire.

"The Monbriths?" Ibram repeated. He furrowed his eyebrows. "What about them? I sent in that report two months ago."

"I don't think I was supposed to say that," Ahksell winced. He looked out the window, squinting. "Let's talk about the view instead."

Ibram poked him in the arm; Ahksell poked him back. The aerial gondola swayed upwards.

"You have to be the worst Attendant Yseult's ever produced," Ibram declared. "Not only have you never been in a fight in your life, you're also the least discreet man I've ever known."

Alchemists were supposed to be like cooks, hoarding their secret recipes and only releasing their by-products for a neat profit. Being the seventh preceptory, Yseult should have been more anxious than most to protect its secrets, yet its members were far more likely to play down their alchemical craft and stress their emphasis on physical education. Ibram had once heard Lady Azadiya declare that all anyone needed to join Yseult was the ability to dance.

It was just a smokescreen, really, to make them seem as approachable as an alchemist could be. Yseult tended to act as a kind of catch-all for the day-to-day affairs of the villages and farms that lay within the Imperial boundary which separated the Sect of Seven Fires from its more commonplace neighbors. Non-specific requests for mediation between angry competitors or a local investigation that no one wanted to bother a warder over always made their way to Lady Azadiya's desk somehow. That was where Ibram and the rest of Ladyship's agents came in, supplying discreet and professional service of whatever type might be needed.

"Oh now, that's not fair," Ahksell said. "I've been in a fight."

Ibram snorted. "Running around the apple orchard being chased by bees is not a fight."

Ahksell shrugged. "Anything you can walk away from."

Ibram frowned down at his feet. What could Ladyship want to know about the Monbriths that he hadn't written in his report? It had been a very cut and dried case, if he recalled correctly. An old man—an itinerant blacksmith—had died, and Ibram had been sent out as a courtesy to the headwoman of the village to make sure everything was above board. The Monbriths had owned the draughtshop where the body had been found. It had all seemed rather mundane, to be sure.

He rubbed his thumb against his eyebrow. The thought that Lady Azadiya might be displeased with him made the back of his neck tighten in stress. Officially, he was employed by the Sect and merely attached to this particular preceptory, but in practice he was...well, in a way he was an illegal legacy hire. His mother had been an agent for the Preceptory of Yseult as he was now, and his father and sister were artisans who mostly took commissions from the Sect of Seven Fires. Alchemists were forbidden by imperial law from having personal retainers; Ibram preferred to think of it as a grey area.

The swaying gondola swung to a gently rolling stop at the clearing station outside the preceptory. Two workers caught each side of the carriage and then pulled it along the short track to the disembarking platform before the next arriving gondola could smash into them. The platform conductor raised both hands and came up to the door to unhook the lock. Ibram lunged for freedom first and stood on the thick wooden beams, breathing the crisp mountain air. It smelled like hot metal and tree sap; he sneezed.

"It's the same air in the gondola, you know," Ahksell said.

"I don't believe you," Ibram muttered. He continued to breathe deeply.

The workers ignored them, already towing the empty gondola out of the way of the next one approaching. Ibram jerked his head, and then he and Ahksell stepped off the platform and down the broad stone stairway that lead to the compound proper. Ahead of them lay the huge metal and granite gates of the preceptory, opened to all visitors, but guarded by gigantic sparking lodestones set into the walls in a diamond pattern. Ama had told him once, when Ibram was a child, that the lodestones were infused with lightning, in such great amounts as to put the security locks folk put on their valuables to shame. She claimed invaders laying siege to Yseult would find a very lively welcome, but now that he was older Ibram didn't put much stock into it. No one had laid siege to so much as a rebellious hamlet in centuries, after all.

Ahksell fell into step with him once they passed through into Yseult, a courtesy which Ibram silently appreciated in deference to his own shorter legs. The Preceptory of Yseult resided in the lowest section of the sect's complex, for which placement, Ibram thanked Yilka the Green daily. A man still had to conquer the steep gradient of the lower sect courtyard to gain access to the interior, but at least Ibram had never gotten a nosebleed out of it. A few other agents of the sect greeted him as Ibram walked through, and bowed to Ahksell in passing. The sun was out, but not yet powerful enough to make its heat felt. Ibram tugged on his high collar and brushed a hand down the sect badge on his chest. His stomach gurgled.

"Here," Ahksell said. He dug into his belt pouch and then held out a wax paper bag full of crystalized ginger.

Stiff breezes ruffled Ibram's hair as he walked; he tucked the loose strands behind both ears. Ibram swallowed heavily. The trip up the living mountain always sent his stomach writhing, and only time had managed to reduce his queasiness to a level where he could mostly ignore it. Ahksell held the bag out and shook the contents. With a groan, Ibram grabbed the biggest piece of ginger he could feel from the bag, and then popped it into his mouth. They veered right down one of the smaller alleys that branched off from the main stone courtyard.

Yseult was conservative for a preceptory, no strange odors or mysterious outbreaks of dancing fever, and only the occasional unexpected explosion. It sprawled with training fields and wooden pavilions, stone dormitories and work buildings, and several garden manors responsible for feeding the mentors, attendants, learners and support staff who lived there. He glanced up at the First Mentor's manor house as they passed by and sucked on his ginger meditatively. A honeycomb manor was probably meant to make visitors from below feel at home when they arrived, but an entire palace raised out of the mountain, whole-cloth, without seam or joint? It just didn't seem altogether friendly.

He bit into the ginger and chewed the fibers, swallowing down the burn. His stomach grumbled to itself. Ibram nodded at the soldier standing guard outside the miniscule Scribes' Bureau tucked into the shadow of the other buildings. All the preceptories had them, a small nod to the empire's continuing interest. The guard nodded back, and then Ahksell had taken the corner and disappeared, which forced Ibram into a walk that could have been called a run in order to catch up.

"Why does Ladyship want the Monbrith report again?" he asked.

Ahksell's head wobbled left and then right. "She didn't say," he replied finally. "But I would wager it has something to do with the runners they sent up late last night."

Ibram paused until he remembered the name of the village. "Runners from Fontis?"

Ahksell guided them down the tree-lined path that led

away from the main buildings. "One of them came up around the evening meal," he said, and then lowered his voice. "But the other had an Imperial badge worked in silver on his chest. He went straight to the Preceptory of Salacia."

Ibram glanced up at that, and caught Ahksell looking just as grim as he felt. The Imperial falcon in silver meant the Bureau of Justice and its Cohorts of Peace and Vigilance. Not the typical visitor up the living mountain at all. The sect was officially a loyal Vissilian guild, of course, but no one wanted an Imperial embarrassment on their back terrace. They walked past the training grounds in silence.

"Has Lady Sebbina requested a visit?" Ibram asked as they turned down the little courtyard outside the Attendants dormitories.

"Her Gracious Majesty's most cherished representative has not come up," Ahksell said. He leaned in closer, which was a bit like being loomed over by a boulder. "But Salacia's Second Mentor has been down the mountain since the first runner came to see Mentor Hobon and *she* has been in her office—oh, shh!"

❧

Look out for the first full-length novel in The Alchemist's Agent series: The Gilty Party *coming soon!*

Interested in following along with Ibram, Lady Azadiya, and the rest of the denizens of the Sect of Seven Fires? Sign up for my monthly newsletter, and receive a new short story!

ABOUT THE AUTHOR

E. M. Burnham likes fantasies, mysteries, and stories of all shapes and sizes, which is why she's decided to write them all at once. She's been a Jedi, a Fellow of The Ring, a Trekker, and even a Newsie, raised on Agatha Christie with a shot of Dorothy L. Sayers and a chaser of Margery Allingham. *Curse-bird On A Wire* is her first published novella.

She has lived and worked on three continents (and somehow earned two masters degrees in the midst of all that moving!) but settled down to be near her family in the United States. You can subscribe to her newsletter to keep up to date on her other work at emburnham.com

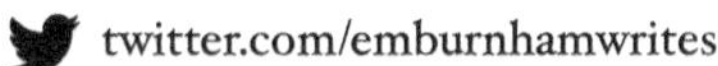 twitter.com/emburnhamwrites

ACKNOWLEDGMENTS

Grateful thanks to Peggy McShane and Ivy Smith for their resourceful editing expertise, and to all my alpha readers. Any mistakes in this book are most assuredly mine.

9 798985 095210